THE KILLER GENE

MARVIN THOMAS

Order this book online at www.trafford.com
or email orders@trafford.com

Most Trafford titles are also available at major online book retailers.

Print information available on the last page.

ISBN: 978-1-4907-7287-5 (sc)
ISBN: 978-1-4907-7286-8 (e)

Library of Congress Control Number: Pending

Trafford rev.   04/22/2016

Trafford www.trafford.com
PUBLISHING

North America & international
toll-free: 1 888 232 4444 (USA & Canada)
fax: 812 355 4082

CHAPTER ONE

Clayton was having difficulty accepting the idea. He had always felt that he wanted to pass on s his own genes, not rely on a stranger to supply his. It just didn't seem "right". It was not a religious thing as he would classify himself as a "severe agnostic". But Gloria had become ever more insistent on their discussing it. They did have their own child, a lovely three year old girl who did seem to be developing a bit slowly and the pediatrician had told them she was "mildly challenged intellectually". That was a diplomatic way, Gloria had insisted, of telling them that their child was a bit "mentally retarded".

"Clay, honey. I know you read that pamphlet I gave to you about the sperm donor center. We can actually choose who we want. I mean, it's like a "made to order" thing. I...just don't want to take another chance on having a "problem" that we have with Linda. I know, obviously, that it may be partly my doing but still…"

Clayton looked at his wife with an impassioned expression. How to deal with this? He adored his wife. She was bright, vivacious and quite beautiful. They had been married for five years and for the most part, it had been most satisfying His daughter was the "apple of his eye", a truly beautiful little girl. But, God, what had happened? They had noticed from the age of six months that she just seemed to be a little slower than other children of the same age. That seemed even more obvious as she grew older. But she had such a "cute" personality everyone would tell them. Clayton agreed but he was still bothered by her slow mental development. But was that enough to go through with what Gloria was suggesting? Did she think the next child would be the same as Linda? What were the real odds?

"Gloria, how do you know that the next child will have any difficulties or, for that matter, a child from a donor won't have any problems?"

"We don't. But, look, we can really check out their list of donors. You can be so thorough that you can almost predict what you will get. We can choose a possible Einstein."

"You really believe that, don't you?"

"Clay, you know how I have researched this. I think the idea of choosing a donor is exciting. Even if I knew our next child would be all right I'd still consider it."

"Yea, it's OK for you to say that. But, genetically, it won't be my child. Have you really taken that fact into account?"

"Clay, honey, I understand that. You think it early won't be yours. But how does that differ from adopting? The genes are not all there is. While they are not all of yours or mines, we can still love their child as if she were totally their own. You know that is the case so often."

Clayton valued her opinions. She was a successful lawyer, graduating in the top ten percent of her law school class. He had met her in college where he was a graduate student at the Business School, seeking his MBA. A mutual friend who was married to one Gloria's fellow students had arranged a date after Clay had told her he wanted to meet that very attractive "legal shark" Their first date had gone well. He had taken her to one of the finer Italian restaurants in the city as he was told that she was quite fond of that cuisine. They seemed to find a number of things in common including, strangely perhaps, a real taste for movies seen at the theater and not by renting a video or the new cds that were now appearing. The food was quite excellent and Gloria took a liking to Clay almost from the start.

He offered her some of his background: From a suburb outside of San Francisco, where he eventually planned to rerun after he received his MBA degree. He was gearing towards management and hoped to find a position in a relatively young firm in which both could... She thought that sounded quite ambitious. Their conversation steered in various directions with an inchoate admiration floating above it all. She thought him quite handsome, moving with that graceful athleticism that she felt was quite masculine.

He was quite surprised when she seemed to welcome his subtle advances which ended up in first date sex. He didn't know what to make of that but their relationship firmed up rapidly. She told him she was from Minnesota but wasn't really planning to return there. She had always thought she might prefer living in New York or another large city on the East Coast while hinting that she was not adverse to the West Coast.

They continued to date almost exclusively that year. It so happened that it was the final academic year for both. One night after dinner and a movie, sitting in his apartment when, looking at him whimsically, she asked him to come to her hometown of St Cloud to meet her parents. He was admiring, as he usually did, her beauty that he noticed solicited glances from other men when they were out together which mad him both proud and a bit possessive, "If you and I are getting serious, and I think we are" she told him "I want you to know them and them you."

Clay studied her carefully. Over the past few months he had thought he had been able to gauge her comments reasonably well, whether they were of a serious or less significant import. She had a clever but occasionally annoying manner of being able to manipulate with her words. Now, she sounded dead serious. He knew he had to measure his words carefully but he also knew he was in love with her. He had felt that sort of giddiness that adolescents feel towards the opposite sex which, of course, wasn't really love. He had this feeling with other women but this was different, very different. It seemed to be "in the marrow". Indescribable, really, but he felt it.

"I have no problem with that" he told her. "When are you thinking?"

"Soon. I just think we need do this soon"

Three weeks later, they were off to St Cloud. He would miss just one or two classes which he felt he could handle. The flight went smoothly. Her home, rather nice twos tory brick and stucco building, was alongside the Angushire Golf Course. Clay usually felt comfortable ion his own skin and therefore had no trouble with the routine but compulsory introductions.

"Mom, Dad, this is Clay Lawrence. He is the guy you have sooo much bout these past few months.:

Clay picked up on the "sooo" an d guessed she had been in considerable communication with them about him already.

"I hope all of it has been good. I am delighted to meet you. Gloria speaks so highly of both of you often and I can see why"

It sounded smooth. Gloria was impressed. So were her parents and the rest of the visit went very well. Both of them were articulate and well-read and Clay really did enjoy the time with them. He learned from Gloria that they were also thrilled with him. Her mother, as it turned out, was an excellent cook and her father a swine connoisseur. If one picks their mate on the basis of their parents, this was a sure thing, he thought.

It was a few weeks after they returned to campus that Clay proposed. The answer was almost instantaneous. "OH, yes,

Clay. Absolutely, yes! I do love you. My parents loved you and I am so excited about this. I know this is the last year of school for us both. I've talked with my parents about your desire to return to the San Francisco area."

While they knew she had not planned to return to St. Cloud and had considered New York or Boston, Clay was fairly well set on the Baby area and she knew how he loved that space. He was surprised how easy it we for her to switch from one coast to the other.

"Clay, I have no problem with San Francisco. I've been there a couple of times and I did love it. But damn, isn't it rather pricey?"

"It is that, sweetheart but we can find someplace not so expensive at first. Plenty of neat places like that. Then, hopefully, when we get situated and rolling in the bucks we can move up. Happens a lot, heh?"

Gloria looked at him and smiled. He was certainly very self-confident. Self-confident and gorgeous. What else would a woman want? And good in bed. Even more then, what would a woman want.

"That is one the things I absolutely adore about you, Clay. Full steam ahead. I agree. Right on. Let's go for it!" They embraced with a solid show of affection sprinkled with considerable passion. He carefully removed her clothing and she I his and in seconds they were engaged in the most satisfying intimacy they had yet experienced."

CHAPTER TWO

They had a simple but elegant wedding. Clay was was not religious and while Gloria was a distant Catholic, she still wanted 'what every woman dreams of: a real wedding with all the bells and whistles:". Gloria's parents had no problem with that and in fact her mother was thrilled to be able to participate with her daughter in the planning. Gloria had one sibling, a brother who was a successful physician back in St. Cloud who had married a woman from Virginia. Gloria's mother had very little involvement in that wedding and looked forward to this one with much anticipation. Clay had learned a bit more about his future mother –in law since their engagement. Her name was Roberta but she went by the nickname of "Billy". She attended the University of Minnesota, planning to be a teacher. Graduating with honors from high school it had been felt by many that she was headed for success regardless of the path she chose. She indeed was doing well and while thinking of a possible career in law or medicine she knew that was a difficult road for women in her era. Then, she met Gloria's father, a play-boy by his own admission and president of his fraternity. Clever, but not an intellectual, he had taken her by storm from the beginning. Clay was surprised to learn that her mother was pregnant before their wedding and being a reasonably observant Catholic knew that abortion was not for her. George, while also a Catholic but not as observant, agreed with her decision. He was a senior in Liberal Arts, and while the thought of going on to business school was considered he told her he would marry her, and, if she wished, return to St Cloud to live. From a small town in Minnesota he would have no problem with that. So, they were married when she was two months pregnant and consequently had been able to keep that a secret for many years. Billy always wondered why her parents, as well as others, couldn't count. George had told her he was sure they could but everyone just left it at that.

Clay admitted later that he "endured" the ceremony. It was a bit longer than he had wished. Growing up a s a Presbyterian, he had not been exposed to all of the rituals of Catholicism. Lengthy stuff, he thought. But his mother and father had travelled from the Bay area and heartily approved of Gloria and her family. They told him later that they had no problem with all the pomp and circumstance of a Catholic ceremony. Frank had asked his future brother-in-law to be his Best Man. He had found him to be a little more distant and reticent than he would have expected relative to the other family members. He was tall but not particularly attractive. Intelligent but rather condescending which irritated Clay more than he wished to admit. He seemed to have this plastic sneer that was almost robotic. But he was able to communicate with him. He was also happy they would not be living in the same time. The reception was also simple but rather elegant. He had recently been to a Jewish phantom where he was amazed to see how elaborate it had been. He did not realize that a full course meal, alcohol, dancing and interminable speechmaking. This was nothing like that. But this was more familiar and suited him quite well.

His mother, Carole, a rather plumb but still rather attractive woman in her late fifties was quite good at social interaction. Friendly and surprisingly well-informed, she could carry a decent conversation with most. She was an avid reader of newspapers and recently taken up with the ATLANTIC MONTHLY and THE NATION. The latter seemed well fitted to her liberal views. She had not attended college, due primarily to financial difficulties but had told Clay more than once that "getting a good education" was paramount. His father, Ralph, a successful accountant was more taciturn. Much more conservative than his wife had led him to frequent disagreement over political questions which had led him to measure his choice of conversational topics. Nevertheless they seemed to have a happy marriage and his memories of his childhood were quite positive. He never was quite sure where either one stood in terms of any religious tenets. They never discussed it much and Clay had always felt looseness about religion in his house although they claimed to be Presbyterian and on occasion they would attend church services. This was more so with his mother. Actually, as he had thought about it, Gloria didn't seem too immersed in Catholicism as long as he had known her he did not remember her going to either Mass or confession ever. She talked a bit about her parents moderate views" of the Church but still, she said, they were practicing Catholics and so, this traditional wedding.

In the midst of the reception, Carole walked over to them as they stood holding a glass of wine and had just finished a conversation with a class mat of Gloria who had been in her wedding party.

"Gloria, if I haven't already said it, you look absolutely stunning today"

"Well, thank you, Mrs. Lawrence."

"Please, Gloria, it's really not Mrs. Lawrence now. Please call me Carole"

"Carole it is. As a matter of fact, I guess I am also Mrs. Lawrence now"

With that, Carole and Gloria shared one of those impromptu small laughs that must happen between a new bride and her mother-in-law as part of the marriage ritual. Gloria genuinely admired Frank's mother. She was intelligent and personable. There may be differences between us in the future, she thought. But now, peace.

"I hear you and Clay will be returning to the Bay area after you both finish school."

Yes, it looks that way. I am excited, really. San Francisco is one of my favorite cities."

Carole smiled. She had found Gloria to be personable and obviously quite intelligent.

"I know you will be graduating Law School. Isn't there a bushel full of lawyers in Frisco? Will that be a problem?"

"I sure hope not Carole. I am going to talk to the dean, He happens to be from there and might be of some help to me."

"Well, of course Clay also has to find himself a job. I know he's put out feels to a number of companies that interest him. But I know he's talented and I know that should not be a problem."

Ordinarily, that would have come across to Gloria as a bit of elite stuffiness. But Carole seemed too genuine for that. She really did feel Clay was talented. Smiling to herself, she silently agreed.

CHAPTER THREE

Shortly after the end of the school year, when Gloria received her JD Degree and Clay his MBA, they made the move to San Francisco. Gloria had spoken to the Law School Dean, who in fact knew of several groups in the Bay area. She had earlier flown pout to the City to and interviewed with two of the firms that appealed to her and finally, after discussing it with Clay settled on the group that already employed two female lawyers. She thought that might make things easier. Having being interviewed by two of the senior partners who were aware of the fact she had graduated in the top ten percent of her class from a prestigious, their response was prompt and positive. Clay had not found a position but had interviewed with several companies. He was not sure what he was looking for but felt it would be challenging to hook up with a relatively new enterprise, one that would allow him to grow along with it. He was confident that his degree from a good business school would serve him well. Gloria agreed with this train of thought., never doubting his ability, confidence and intelligence.

Gloria's starting salary was more than either of them had expected, enabling them to rent a reasonably nice apartment just north of the City. Frank continued interviewing with those who asked him to do so after reviewing his resume. Finally, after what seemed to Clay to be a most frustrating adventure, given his self-confidence he met with a small company involved with a new style of search engines for computer software. This was exactly the sort of thing he was looking for: a relatively young company with some terrific new ideas about today's technology with hopes for an even better tomorrow. Unfortunately the starting salary for the position was not as high as he wished. But Gloria was very supportive, perhaps as she was going to do better than he. That was a bittersweet thought. But the challenge of this opportunity was palpable and he accepted.

Their life seemed to glide into a rhythm recognizable to may suburbanites. They had settled into a rather comfortable apartment not far from the Golden Gate Park. Gloria was adjusting to San Francisco even though she thought the rent for this apartment, small but adequate, was rather exorbitant. San Francisco was turning out to be just what she had heard: very cosmopolitan and politically liberal. She was comfortable in this setting. She found the restaurants to be interesting, many very good, and some, excellent. The cost of living in the City certainly was a challenge but her job was providing adequate compensation, enabling her and Clay to do what they wanted, albeit with some compromises. Clay was surprisingly satisfied with his choice of companies. The President and Vice=president, both of whom she had met when Clay and her were invited to the president's home for dinner and conversation, were young, smart, and very aggressive. They both expressed their opinion that Clay was the dynamic addition they had been looking for and were certain he would share in what they predicted would be a very successful operation.

It was a typical evening at home when Gloria first broached the subject. She liked to cook initially, somewhat of a surprise to Clay, and as it turned out, also to his delight, she was quite good at it. Her maturing years in St Cloud featured watching her mother's culinary skills which she felt were rather extraordinary. This meal consisted of veal scaloppini with marsala sauce and mushrooms, one of his favorites. An added penne pasta topped off with a bottle of their favorite pinot noir was a superb choice.

"Clay, hone y. Have you thought about a family?" She looked at him with that question mark of a face that women are able to mold so ably. She was as beautiful in this pose as any other and he always enjoyed her visage.

"Not much I guess, why?"

"Well, when do you think we should start?"

"Honey, we've only been married for ten, months"

"But I think things are going well, don't you?"

"Yes" he answered without hesitation.

"Then why not"

He looked at her carefully. He knew, by now, when she was quite serious.

"Well, for one, raising a child in this day and age is a bit expensive. It will also interfere with our lifestyle to a great extent. Don't get me wrong, Gloria. I have every intention of having a family. The question is is when, not if"

"Clay, I know all of that. Of course it will interfere with our life style. It is supposed to! I have talked with my firm and they have no problem with the female lawyers having children. We get a six week maternity leave and then I can return to work. Two of the women just had babies within the past year or so are back to work on a fairly regular basis. I know I am twenty-six and my biological clock is still running but I just have this feeling that now is the time."

Clay had no problem with the idea of a family. While he was not certain he could see himself as a doting father and looked at the change in life style as questionable, he had this innate feeling of passing on his genes. It was more than just a subconscious thought. He had pondered it frequently over the past year or two.

"I can see you are rather serious about this, aren't you, honey?" he looked t her with an expression of both understanding and inquiry.

"Yes" was her simple but solid answer. She left him with no doubt as top her feelings about this.

"All right, Gloria. I really do not have a big problem with this. I gather you are ready to give up your birth control pill?"

"Silly. Of course. I have already stopped them. Haven't taken any for the past month."

Clay just could not get angry over this and her remark actually evoked spontaneous chuckles form them both.

She looked so radiant this night and all of this led to a rather heighted intimacy which after and she lay next to him brought the thought that this was certainly a bonus to his rather quick agreement

CHAPTER FOUR

He had forgotten about that conversation they had had that night. He did notice that their frequency of sex had increased. Whether that was w reward for his compliance or not seemed irrelevant under the circumstances. She had bonded much better with his mother than he thought possible and the four of them frequently spent time together. Gloria was also gaining an admirable reputation at her law firm as both capable and very bright. Additionally, he was more satisfied with his career choice that he thought would be the case. The formula behind the business was clever and innovative and becoming well known and successful. They told him he was playing a significant role in its expansion and success and he had been rewarded with two raises already. While his compensation was still a bit less than Gloria, he was close enough now to feel more comfortable with the remaining disparity.

He remembered it as a Wednesday evening. They had decided to go to one of their favorite restaurants in the City. Since it was a very fine French eatery, they knew a comparable fine wine needed to accompany their meal.

"Let's order a really expensive one, honey" Gloria suggested.

"Why? Is this night different from other nights or what?" Clay responded

"Yes, it is different"

Clay looked at his wife with a bit of wonderment,

"Because....I am pregnant." She answered with just a hint of a smile that widened as she looked at him.

He got up from his chair, walked over to her and gave him a kiss on her cheek. "That is wonderful, honey. When did you find out?" he asked as he sat once again.

"Thank, you, Clay, for that little show of affection and support. I appreciate it very much."

"Gloria, you know I am very much in favor of having children. My only contention has been the timing. I really am delighted. When did you find out?""

Actually, just today. I am three weeks late and I am usually rather regular. There is an obstetrician in our building whom I've met and like so I just went t to see her. She confirmed it."

"Well, let's get the waiter over here and order a very expensive wine indeed. You probably won't be drinking too much after this anyway."

A fine bottle of Bordeaux was chosen which by the end of their meal was completely emptied.

Her pregnancy went relatively well. Frank's mother was supportive and helpful. She was at her office on most days, the occasional absence due to variable degrees of nausea. A rising star at the firm, the partners quite satisfied with her work, telling her more than once she would be missed during her maternal leave but they recognized how excited she was about having her first child. All made her feel comfortable and secure with her position.

Clay was equally delighted with how well things were going for him. Both the CEO and his assistant were young and very energetic. They had been able to market their products with both enthusiasm and surprising aplomb. With a good deal of responsibility delegated to him, Clay had responded with equal enthusiasm and proven competence. A bonus had been promised within six months of his start, again helping him in his relationship with his wife. Why the difference in income continued to trouble him was not always clear. He was not of the old male patronizing school and realized she was, after all, a professional with an advanced degree somewhat beyond d his. He loved being back in San Francisco I and was thrilled that Gloria was becoming more enchanted with the area as time went by. Life seemed good. Their sex life had slowed down a bit as her pregnancy advanced but she was very imaginative, determined to satisfy him.

He was in the midst of a relatively unimportant meeting when his phone rang on a sunny Thursday afternoon. His office overlooked the Bay, an obviously enormous plus, and he found the sight of water relaxing as well as contemplative. Knowing that her due date was now very close, he kept his cell phone on constantly. Great invention, that cell phone, he thought but the reverse side of the coin was its constant intrusion into one's life. The vibration startled him.

:"Excuse me" he uttered as he quickly picked up the phone to answer.

She told him the contractions had started.

He paused for a moment then continued: "I think we should get a move on, huh?I can get home in. OK, you already talked to her and she'll drive you to the hospital. Great. I'll meet you there soon. Keep cool, babe. I know you will"

Turning to the others in the room, a smile crossed his facds.

"I think you all know we are expecting our first. She is going into labor now, I guess, so."

He was stopped in mid-sentence "I think we all understand, Clay. We can finish this at a later date. Go, man, and good luck to both of you."

"Thanks all. I'll try to keep you up to date" he said as he arose to leave.

He told his secr4etary on the way out why he was leaving but by then the small office knew the reason for his departure. He thought about how this time of one's life, the birth of a child unites humanity in some sort of bond that most endorse and others, while not rejecting, just ignore. Here, it was a joyful binding. He reciprocated with thankful acknowledgement as he left.

He drove with some urgency but he did not want to be stopped for speeding nor get involved in an accident that would delay him. Arriving at the hospital, he surprisingly found a parking space rather easily. After entering the main floor, he was instructed to the obstetrics area. It was easy to find and having given his name, was led into the waiting room. Gloria had just arrived and was being examined. He would be allowed to see her momentarily.

When he walked into her room, she was already in a hospital gown.

"I seem to be dilating well, honey," she told him "It is definitely time"

"Good, I think we are both ready"

Leaning over to kiss her, he took a seat by her bed. Her labor was something prolonged but only mildly painful. About ten hours later, she was wheeled off to the delivery room. Clay was the usual impatient father-to be, pacing but confident. His mother had called three times and asked if she was needed. He told her it best that she wait at home and she agreed.

He was relieved when the obstetrician came in to see him.'

Everything is fine, Mr. Lawrence. Your wife is great and you have a new baby girl."

CHAPTER FIVE

Linda was the name her mother had suggested. Both of them liked it and neither did Clay's parents but Clay wondered if the fact that it was not their idea meant anything to them. He hoped not. He did not want any "in-law" factors entering into their marriage. So far none had but as with all couples, he hoped they never would. But that might have been wishful thinking.

Linda seemed to be exhibiting and acting like any baby. The pediatrician did not say he felt anything amiss when she had her three month's check. Clay thought, like all fathers must, that she was beautiful. He believed it more so when strangers seemed to go out of their way to tell him. Gloria had returned to work after six weeks and they were able to afford a nanny for the day.

Both he and Gloria as well as the nanny and his parents thought she was progressing as expected but by the third month, the nanny started to make oblique comments that made Gloria concerned. She did not think Linda was quite where she should be physically. When Gloria told her pediatrician about what was said, she told that these remarks were probably a "bit premature". While she might be a bit slow it was too early to say this was not a normal progression.

At six months, none of them had any doubts that Linda seemed to be slower than she should have been. Pressed by Gloria, the pediatrician became more frank.

"Yes, Mrs. Lawrence. I would have to agree. She is a bit slow for her age."

"Is that the way it's going to be? I mean, how slow? She certainly isn't retarded."

"No of course not. That is much too harsh of a word to use here. A little slower than I would like but certainly not retarded."

"So, what can we expect?"

"I'm sorry, what do you mean?"

"I mean what we can expect. Will she need to go to a special school?? Can she be self-sufficient? I think you know what I mean."

The pediatrician, a middle-aged woman with large glasses and a hairdo that Gloria thought made her look matronly., nevertheless was, in her mind, quite competent and in whom she had a great deal of confidence. Helen was her name. She had a good bedside manner and related well to both the child and parent.

"I do, Mrs. Lawrence." She responded with no change in her expression.

"Doctor, please call me Gloria, will you? It sounds a little less formal."?

"Of course, Gloria. I appreciate your concern. It would be abnormal I guess if you did not have it. I know you are a very successful l lawyer and your husband, you have told me, is quite talented. You cannot believe a child of yours could be slow in any way."

Gloria knew, of course, that she had seen other children just like this and knew more or less what to say to the parents, which was the important part of her diplomacy as a pediatrician.

"I cannot believe it, yes. I thought the laws of genetics were fairly predictable."

"Don't we wish. Listen, you are jumping a bit ahead. Linda is a beautiful child and will probably do very well as time goes on. She probably will not need any special school but may need a little more help than others."

"Thank you, Doctor. I'm sorry if I've acted…I guess elitist here. She is my daughter and I love her. I guess I was hoping…" her voice trailed off. She didn't know if she was too embarrassed or guilty to finish the sentence.

Over the next two years, Gloria resigned herself to what the fates had brought. While she thought she was handling it well and was bonding in a fashion that she thought was quit normal with her daughter, there was always that feeling of betrayal. While nominally a Catholic, she did not really attend Mass that often and did not feel this was a punishment from God. She knew Clay was an agnostic and she never discussed the religious aspects of all of this., if there really was any in her mind. She continued tp work regularly and was felt to be the rising star of her law office. Clay was now a vie-president and widely respected both in his firm and by a number of other informational technology companies in the area. Their combined incomes were steadily accelerating.

They had kept Linda's nanny as the two of them had formed a mutual bond. The nanny, a buxom woman in her fifties named Hillary, was pleasant and helpful both to Linda and them. She had recognized Linda's limitations and was working with her to help develop some basic motor skills. Clay, as had Gloria, had resigned himself to her shortcomings but adored her. She was a beautiful child and aside from her 'slowness' had a very outgoing personality that seemed to please all who met her.

It was at this time that Gloria began to discuss her desire for another child but to use a sperm donor.

Clay had been very resistant and remained that way. Gloria was on contraceptives and even though she wanted that second child hinted to him, they would not have unprotected sex. He was resentful of her attitude and knew this was the beginning to drive a wedge between them. It was one of those evenings when they were in bed that she had leaned over. Noticing no arousal, she became a bit dismayed.

"Clay, what in the hell is the matter?"

He lay there, saying nothing for several minutes. Finally: "I'm pissed, Gloria, to be honest."

"About my desire for a sperm donor?"

"Yes"

"Clay, sweetheart, I love you very much. In many ways this has nothing to do with you. This will not be our last child, I hope. But I must test it just this once to be sure. I need you to understand."

"Clay was having great trouble comprehending the meaning of this conversation. Was Gloria implying that she feared it was his fault that Linda was like she was? Was she "experimenting" with the second child to try to clear this concern? Clay had accepted the importance of "passing on his genes" if you will and it seemed to him this was a refutation of this by his wife. He certainly loved her but this was definitely putting a strain on their marriage. It clearly had cooled their sexual ardor, which had been exciting to both of them, and that too was disturbing.

"Sweetheart" he answered, trying not to show too much anger but only "angst". "I am trying to understand but it isn't easy. You are making it seem Linda's problem, which I think we are exaggerating, is my fault."

." Clay, don't be silly. It may be just as much mine. But this is a way for me at least help solve a problem I have. Trust me, I want more than two children and this is the only time I would ever propose anything like this"

"Really, Gloria. Don't you think this whole idea of yours is a bit bizarre? I mean, we are BOTH capable of producing another child for Christ's sake!"

Gloria looked at him in a more stern way than he had ever noticed. She always seemed quite rational to Clay but now. but now.

"I know that, Clay. I do not think this is bizarre. I do not want to take another chance right now. Please let me go through with this."

Clay was truly in a quandary. Morally, he did not think this was correct. Not in a religious moral sense but in amore humanistic sense. He also felt insulted and belittled. He was, he thought, a strong personality but this was difficult for him to accept. But Gloria seemed adamant about it, however, And maybe it was wise to let this happen. He did, he admitted to himself, harbor a few doubts about why this happened to their daughter.

"All right Gloria. It seems you w ant to do this rather badly." He hesitated a bit. Should he go ahead and give his verbal approval. Burt then he finished. "OK. Let's go for it"

Gloria smiled at him and embraced him tightly. Her hand went to his penis again and now, with this seemingly settled, Clay responded.

CHAPTER SIX

Clay was doing his best to accept what had transpired. He was uncertain that he had made the right decision. He could not quite get it out of his mind and it seemed to be affecting his work. He needed to speak with someone else about and unscramble his thoughts. He ruled out discussing this with any of his colleagues at work. While he did feel 'spiritual', he was not what he felt was formally religious and did not feel the need to seek clerical guidance. There was uncertainty of discussing this with his parents, although both of them were quite logical and reasonable. With this uncertainty leaving him rudderless, he decided to call them. He would simply tell them there was something he wished to discuss, alone.

He arranged to have dinner with them on a night that Gloria had na office meeting and the nanny was available to stay with Linda. Gloria thought that was just perfect:

Clay spending the evening with his parents while she was away. The drive to their home was a bit of an effort. He was using the time to construct his approach to the subject. He didn't know why he was so uneasy. It just seemed, well, unnatural.

"Clay, honey:" was his mother's greeting as she walked out of the door to meet him in the driveway. "I am so glad you could make it tonight. It seems that we so rarely can just have dinner with you alone anymore. Just like old times."

"Has that been a problem, mom" Clay asked. He was not certain what she had meant.

"Of course, not, Clay. You know I am not a clinging mother. You aren't supposed to have dinner with us alone that often anymore but when you do, it's such a pleasure to me. Still"

He leaned over and kissed her on her cheek. "Of course you are not clinging. You have been terrific. I am not sure I ever thought that. You are still the love of my life"

She smiled and blushed. "Every mother likes to hear that"

She accompanied him into their home. It was not large, having downsized after the children moved out years ago. It was nicely decorated and was rather contemporary in line with his mother's tastes.

"Ralph, look wh9o's here."

His father still worked every day as an accountant, a rather successful one at that. He seemed to doi t as "his job". Clay never did feel that he really liked what he did. However, they had always had a fairly good relationship and he valued his father's opinion, perhaps more than his mother's, particularly in this situation.

"Good to see you, son. Yes, it is nice to have you alone again, not that we don't enjoy Gloria and Lnda but you know, once in a great while."

"I know what you mean, Dad. It's great for me, too."

They sat down at the table under a lovely chandelier that his mother prized. It was a b it less contemporary that the rest of the house but this she had found several years ago and fell in love with. It was stately and added a certain layer of elegance to the surroundings.

"Wait and see what your mother has made just for you, Clay. I think you are going to like it"

With that, she brought out a platter of meat loaf surrounded by a collection of browned potatoes. Truly, one of his favorites. as only his mother seemingly could concoct. But this was not one of Gloria's favorites so there had been a hiatus between meat loafs, a pity he had always felt.

OK, Mom. You did it. Truly worth the visit alone."

"I know. That's why I made it. Your father loves it too, so it was really an easy choice. And, dah, dah, we opened this simply wonderful bottle of Pinot Noir to go with it."

"Clay buried his portion of meat loaf beneath a mountain of bright red catsup, which was his habit, but enjoying every bite. A generous salad accompanied it and she had constructed a mélange of fresh vegetables to top it all off. It was, as Clay told her, "beyond delicious".

When they finished, Clay pushed his chair back and with some degree of trepidation started the discourse.

"Look, one of the reasons I wanted to be you two alone tonight was to discuss something that is bothering me"

His mother suddenly constructed that façade that Clay recognized immediately: A Mother's look of concern.

"Clay, it's not your marriage, is it?"

Why did he know that would be the first question?

"No, Mom, it's not my marriage. Gloria and I are just fine"

She leaned back in her chair, more serene now.

"Clay I've got your favorite dessert, too. Now or do you want to wait?"

Why she had inserted that question at this point remained a but mysterious to him but undoubtedly she had her purpose.

"Let's wait a bit, Mom. I am a little stuffed"

"Fine, Clay. Now, what is it you want to discuss?"

For the next fifteen minutes, Clay went through the details of his and Gloria's discussions and decisions. He glanced from his mother's face to his father's, attempting to fathom their reaction to what he was telling them. Finally, he simply sat back in his chair, picking at the remains of his meal

As he expected, his mother was the first to reply.

"Interesting, Clay, but, at the same time, I guess I would have to say a bit disturbing. Does she think it's your fault or something? And, I mean, Linda is really not THAT slow"

Clay was not surprised by her comments. He, too, had felt that way initially and to some extent, still did. She seemed a bit angrier than he thought she would be and wondered if this was the thing to do, discuss it with his parents before the actual event occurred.

"No, no, Mother She's not blaming anyone. She knows it just happened, if you will. Her concern, it seems, is that it could happen again and she wants another child. I also think the idea of all of this intrigues her."

"Intrigues her!" his father exclaimed. "What do you mean 'intriguesher'?"

This was as much anger as his father would ordinarily express signifying how this was obviously disturbing him.'

"Well, maybe that isn't the right word. Dad. Shall I say, 'interests her'"

"I'm not sure I can tell the difference"

"Clay, honey. How can you be sure you would get want you think are getting??" his mother broke in, trying, he conjectured, to avoid any major confrontation with his father, which she knew would be a bit unusual for both of them.

"Well, obviously, Mom, nothing is that certain in life. But Gloria has really researched this and feels it is a wonderful opportunity without the risks that." his voice trailed again. Why did Gloria feel that Linda was going to be a burden and that they both deserved so much better and they might not it again? "we might have another problem."

"What the hell problem are you talking about, Clay?" his father thundered.

"Ralph", she again broke in, "I think you know what Clay is talking about. I don't know if it's really that much of a problem but, obviously, Gloria does."

"Listen, son, we take what God gives us. Linda is a terrific little girl and I don't see her as a problem. I'm not stupid. I know what you are referring to but she's only two and for Christ's sake how can we know how she is going to do in the future?"

"Clay, I know you are not a religious person and both your father and I are not fervent either but know, this just doesn't seem natural. Gloria is not infertile now, is she?"

"No, no, Mom. That is not the problem."

"You keep saying 'problem'. Is it really that much of one between the two of you. She seems pretty set on doing this."

"Clay" his father interposed "she is Catholic. That seems out of step with her religion."

"Dad, I don't know whether it is or isn't. Gloria is, I guess, more Catholic in name than substance. She's not felt this is a moral problem. I'm not sure. She is"

There was silence now. It seemed none of them knew what to say next. But his mother, true to form, spoke.

"Clay, you know both your father and I are quite liberal. I think we are both well-read and, if you will, 'wordily'. I am having a problem with this but I know you came here for our thoughts and perhaps, advice. I personally do not think there is a problem and I think you and Gloria should try for another child on your won. But if she is so committed to this it might be a problem with your marriage and, God forbid, something goes wrong. she will never forgive you. So, as your mother, rather than, perhaps an innocent bystander, if you will, I will tell you to go ahead with her plans. I also think that will be very important for you."

Clay looked at his mother with an expression that seemed to meld together both gratitude and relief. His father sat immobile yet, not saying much. Finally, he took up his fork, dawdled with it on his plate and looked intently at him.

"You know, Clay, you have a very wise mother. I am not sure I agree with her but I don't disagree either. I am certainly having trouble with all of this and I hope you are not making a very big mistake. But. your mother makes sense. I agree."

Why is it, Frank thought, that some parents, especially his, can step in at the right time with what seems to be the right answers for that situation. Is this one the benefits of the 'family' if you will?

"Mom…Dad…thanks. I must say this has been somewhat of a difficult time for me. I have not felt I could talk to very many others about this but, well, this worked for me. I feel better about it. And having this meal, Mom, made everything that much better. God was that good!"

CHAPTER SEVEN

Clay and Frank discussed at length what had transpired at his meal with his parents. She had always had a comfortable relationship with her in-laws and was relieved with what he told her but was not surprised. Clay, however, had hedged the suggestion regarding a third child and thought that best left for the future.

"OH, Clay, I am so happy you did go to see them. Maybe we are all on the 'same page' now?"

"I think so" came his reply.

"Great! Now..wow. I am really excited about this, honey. I am really anxious to get in touch with the sperm bank and I..we, can decide on the donor"

While Clay had thought about this for several months and thought he was reconciled to the decision, he still felt uneasy

"You are dead serious about this, right?"

"Dead serious" she promptly responded, leaving no doubt here.

Allright. Listen, Gloria. How do we go about this? It's not a 'new father'. It is simply a 'sperm donor".

"Clay, you are splitting hairs now."

"Yes, I am all right with it. All I am asking is where do we go next with this?"

The next step should be very exciting. I have just glanced at tit but they have, well, I guess you would call it a 'catalog' with photos of all their donors and a rather complete pedigree, essentially."

"Do they list the family histories> I mean, you would like to screen out any genetic disorders."

"Clay, I imagine they would have already done that if they are going to accept you as a donor. But we can be certain when we look into it.

"I assume we will both be involved in this selection process?"

"Of course." Gloria answered, rather tartly. "Did you think you would possibly be left out?"

He sensed the gorge developing in their rock solid marriage. He still loved her deeply and knew he didn't want this to cause a final rupture. By no means.

"No, honey. Not really. You'll have to forgive me if I have been a ittle'rough on the edges'. This is just, well, you know, a bit foreign to me yet."

Gloria came and sat next to him, kissing him on the cheek and holding his hand.

"I know, clay. And you have really been wonderful about it. I love you. I want both of us to be comfortable with this and move ahead. OK?"

Sure. Let's do it. Do what is needed next and let's go."

With that, the embraced with a bit more passio0in that Clay had noticed in the past few weeks. He somehow felt a bit more secure now. 'God, this has been a hell of a decision' he thought.

Clay continued following his usual routine during all of this. His company, in spite of rising completion, was doing quite well and so was he, making a handsome salary with the occasional bonus. He worked well with the top execs of the firm, he seemed to be well liked throughout the office and he had frequently been praised for adding value to the firm. He also found that he was growing closer to Linda. As beautiful as ever, he was adjusting to her pace of development. She relished her time with him and the nanny was always accommodating. They would spend time on the weekends, occasionally without Gloria, and he felt the strengthening of their bond. He realized that she was a very lovable child even though he could not help notice the 'differences'. His parents seemed to want to see her more often now and even they had become more attached. Gloria seemed pleased with all of this which relieved some of his anxiety.

Several weeks after their discussion, Gloria told him that she had contacted the sperm bank. They were eating breakfast with Linda but Clay felt she would not understand this so did not interrupt.

"Clay I called the sperm bank yesterday""

"And"

"I've made an appointment for both of us to meet with them next week. Tuesday morning at 10. Can you arrange your schedule>"

Clay looked at her and then at Linda who was picking at her food like two-year olds are want to do. He wanted, for some reason he could not then determine, simply embrace her.

"Yea, I think so, honey. I have a meeting later in the day but I can swing the 10 o'clock deal"

"Good, I will confirm that time."

The conversation then drifted to the things that every couple seems to be concerned with. Some light, some a bit more involved and even some aimed at the news of the day. They both did their bits to help Linda who continued eating in stuttered fashion. She had mastered the art of feeding herself but there were gaps. Clay noticed a bit of irritation and impatience in Gloria's handling of all of this and he realized

It bothered her more than it did him.

He went to his office a little earlier on that Tuesday morning. Having redecorated it just a few months previously he found a bit of solace, always, in those surroundings. Not that he felt he needed to get away from home but that this environment he had created seemed to suit his physical needs. His secretary, a middle-aged woman of around fifty-two, Lorene by name, was there at the time and knew he had marked himself out from ten until his afternoon meeting at three. He had found d her to be helpful and reliable, two traits that mattered the most to him. And, she was efficient. She had three children, two of them now in their teens, one in his early twenties. Like many women who are also mothers, she was always inquiring s to how Linda was doing. For whatever reason, he had told her the problem and found her to be sympathetic. But he wanted to limit the time in discussing her at this moment.

"Morning, Lorene. Anything I need to know?"

She was always cheerful, too much sometimes, he thought. But better this way.

"Not really, Mr Lawrence. You should have no trouble getting away for that meeting at ten."

"Thanks. I do have some items to clean up before then. I assume the meeting this afternoon is still a go?"

I haven't heard anything different" she responded.

His desk was anything but neat. Lorene thought this was a distinctive mark of a 'creative mind;' of which there were many in this enterprise. Rather compulsively orderly at home, Clay seemed to fell this would seem inappropriate at this place. Gloria thought this was a bit illogical but never told him to change his work habits. He took the time to begin sorting out the things he wanted tod o that day but his mind was elsewhere He was both excited and a bit leery of what was to transpire this morning. Finally, he simply signed the most important papers, handed them to Lorene, and left. They had planned to meet at the Sperm Bank, thinking it foolish to try to meet elsewhere to go together. He drove out of the garage where he parked his car, turned right onto Sutter and headed to Bush St where the meeting would take place.

He had been on this street many times in the past but for whatever reason did not notice the brown building in the middle of the block. A rather non-descript sort of thing, he thought. Maybe they don't want to be conspicuous. There was a public parking garage not far from the building and he entered, luckily found a parking space. Walking out, he noticed Gloria's car. The day was a bit crisp, often like this in the early Fall. People seemed to be everywhere and, as always, it seemed in San Francisco, the putative 'homeless;' on the side of the buildings. The building itself had a simple sign that read 'Reproductive Center' and nothing more. A waiting room was immediately encountered after he opened the door to the office.

"Clay, over here" Gloria motioned to him.

"Hi honey, what's up?"

"I checked in already. No need for you to do anything. They are on schedule so we should be in there in a few minutes."

He sat down next to her. The chairs were surprisingly comfortable for a medical office. He was used to less. Looking around the waiting room, he noticed that they were the only ones there. Before him was a reception counter enclosed behind a glass panel and a middle-aged woman with thick glasses working behind. She didn't even glance up to acknowledge him. There were several etchings on the wall, those tranquillizing types favored in Doctor's offices, the room itself painted a soothing pastel blue.

"How's your day so far, dear?" Gloria asked

"Short. Not much happening really. Did you come right from home or did you stop in your office?"

"Right from home> I didn't need to get tied down with any potential problems. You know how that goes."

"Oh yeh" he answered. "I was lucky. No problems But I'm just a stone's throw from here. Was anybody waiting in here when you arrived?"

"NO. The receptionist told me we should be seeing the doctor soon enough."

Clay nodded and looked around the room again. Nothing on the walls pointed to what went on here. The woman behind the glass seemed totally engrossed in whatever she was doing. As he held Gloria's hand, she turned and smiled affectionally at him. Clay had to admit to himself that this really felt rather strange but before he could dwell on his emotions any further, the lady with the head and glasses got up and opened the sliding window of her little cubicle. She smiled as if she didn't really wish to but that was what one did.

"The doctor will be ready soon." She told them. "please follow me"

The body with the head was trim but wearing a rather plain dress that seemed to capture her essence. She led them down a short hall lined with the sort of paintings one might buy at any discount store. She led them into a room that while small, did not seem crowded. A desk was situated in the middle, as if on an island, atop a carpet that did not seem to have been cleaned for some time. Clay was puzzled at the somewhat shabby nature of the place. He was relieved when the door opened shortly after their arrival. He was growing short on words with Gloria, a bit unusual for him.

In walked a short, pudgy man wearing a white coat, shirt unbuttoned at the top. He wore thick glasses and was balding and looked to be in his early sixties.

Nodding, he asked: "Mr. and Mrs. Lawrence? I am Dr Annenberg" He extended his hand to them and Clay thought his grip strong, reflecting his personality as they say?

"I am sure you have read the information that we sent you about this Clinic and our work?" he asked them.

"Yes I have" Gloria answered.

The doctor nodded approvingly and now locked at Clay.

'And you, Mr. Lawrence, have you also read it? "Implying that maybe he hadn't.

Actually, Clay had only glanced at the information. Thinking about it now, he acknowledged that it was another shadow cast on his desire to go through with this.

"I'm familiar with it" was his his lame answer. He didn't think he should say he really hadn't.

The doctor gave Clay a glance of uncertainty s to what that answer meant.

"Good. Now, then, is there a problem with conception? I see by your history that you have a child."

"Not really" said Gloria. "I see. Have you been trying? I mean, is your frreque4ncy of intercourse changed in any way?"

Clay that was an intriguing question. Let's see how Gloria answers that. Actually, it hadn't.

"No" she answered promptly. 'Well, have you been tested, Mr Lawrence, as to the quantity of your sperm count?"

"No"

Clay wasn't sure i9f the doctor was puzzled or disdainful.

"Well, then. Is there a problem with your child? Mental, physical or both?"

Clay hesitated and was prepared to let Glloria control the conversation at this point.

"Doctor. I…we..feel there is a serious developmental defect, mentally."

"How severe? Is she in an institution?"

Well, no"

"Does she go to school away from home?"

"S he's too young for school, Doctor. She is only three."

Dr,. Annenberg again looked above the glasses that hung loosely on his nose. It was that kind of gaze that Clay felt signaled some confusion and perhaps disapproval. He didn't know but was becoming more uneasy about this meeting. He didn't know how Gloria felt but he knew how he did.

"Mr. and Mrs. Lawrence" he intoned. "I am a bit puzzled. Most peop-0kle who seek donor insemination usually do so because the husband lacks a healthy quantity of sperm or it is a single woman, usually lesbian who does not wish to engage in the usual sexual intercourse to become pregnant. Both those parts seem to be missing here, at least as far as I can tell"

Clay couldn't help but be a bit bemused as the doctor's sense of misunderstanding. He didn't want to to look at

Gloria yet as he felt this may be annoying her. But she didn't wait any longer and was now ready to capture the direction of the inquiry. "Alright, Dr. Annenberg, let me tell you why we are here. I am quite concerned about having another child like Linda. I know things may turn out great for her but I worry. I like the idea of picking a sperm donor with the attributes that we both admire and I think we will not have to take a chance of repeating what has happened. That is why we are here. If that is a problem, then there is no reason for us to continue wasting your time."

Annenberg's lips parted slightly and Clay thought this was the best smile he could give. Somewhat of a peculiar chap, this. "Mrs. Lawrence. I am not usually judgmental and I don't intend to be here or at least seem to be. Don't you think, however, that this may be a bit selfish of you? The chances of repeating what happened are not that great and I's sure your husband feels a bit marginalized by this"

Clay had felt that they had a good marriage with a good rapport. But this was lying over him like a cloud. He was somewhat by Gloria's behavior over the past months but still, he did not want to stand in her way. He didn't know if this was cowardice on his part or some subconscious concern that she was right about another child between them. She seemed so determined about this was like a different person. Was this the woman I married he thought. Oh Christ. What a cliché! Of course this was that woman. But..God, she does seem different to me.

"Doctor, I don't know if this is what you must do before agreeing to proceed but I am quit certain this is what I want to do. So does Clay. Maybe we need to checkout some other facility" Her eyes had narrowed and presented a visage both anger and disappointment.

"No, not really, Mrs. Lawrence. It does seem you are quite determined to go ahead with this."

"Yes, we are."

Clay was wondering what the cost of this was and how profitable for the doctor and his staff but he assumed he didn't want to go elsewhere. Maybe he was cynical but also realistic.

"Doctor, just what does all this cost?"

That thin hint of a smile on his thin lips appeared again.

Clay tried not to look stunned, although he had more or less anticipated an answer like that.

"That's fine, doctor. "Gloria interrupted before Clay could say a word.

"Well, then, let me explain the process. As you know, we have a fairly large catalogue of donors with their complete biography and family history. There is also the result of exams. We feel comfortable about all of them. Once you and your husband have decided, we can determine the date of the insemination."

"Do we…just. Kind of look through that catalog and pick?" Gloria asked.

"Of course. You will do that at any time you wish."

How about now?"

Certainly "he responded.

He directed them to another part of the office, an enclosed room with wood-paneled walls and two speakers in the ceiling that spun out "soft music". It turned out that this was the 'cognitive room', in which one explored the possibilities in the depths of thought. Clay thought this was pretty fucking corny but he was determined. to go along with it even though he knew his heart wasn't into it. An assistant brought in a bulky looking album, bound in leather. She explained that even in this era of computers, Dr Annenberg felt it was more 'personal' the patients to 'feel the contents'. It contained all the information, including, obviously up-to-date photos, to help them make an intelligent choice. A desk and several chairs were provided. Gloria sat and began that ever so important exploration.

"Clay, I'll need your input, you know. After all, this will be your chiuld, too"

He thought about that remark. It was a bit incredulous; It was not his child, really. He did not answer her. Sitting next to her, he watched as she thumbed through the 'catalog'. He thought this was quite an entrepreneurial approach to fatherhood. Actually, it was rather fascinating. On each page was a photograph of the 'candidate' and a rather extensive biography. Among the items listed were the tested IG of each. It also listed their level of education and what college, I f any, they attended and when they graduated and in what. After a few moments, she stopped on one of the pages.

"Look, Clay, this one looks quite interesting."

He slid the book over for a better view. The photograph was of a man who was listed at 32 years of age. Rather handsome with a slightly dark complexion which highlighted his looks. He had graduated from Princeton in political science and then went on to Harvard Law School. He was listed as a practicing attorney.

"Impressive" was his immediate response.

"I thought so, too"

The biography also included his health history and that of his family. Nothing of concern there. "Clay, this is the one. I feel it. I really do."

"Fine, Gloria. If that's what you want, fine."

"Now, how do we..are we done? I guess we'll just open the door and find someone"

"I guess "Clay opened the door, stepped out into the hall and walked towards the reception desk. He told her 'they had chosen'

"Good" the lady with the artificial smile answered. "I'll tell Dr. Annenberg. Just wait in the room with your wife."

"Thanks, I will"

Returning to the room, he noticed Gloria still thumbing through the 'catalog'.

"I thought you..we had decided on Mr. Harvard"

"I have but I wanted to keep looking. I am even more certain now, Clay"

Dr Annenberg walked in about fifteen minutes later, smiling in his inimitable fashion which Clay had now registered.

"Betty says that you have made your choice. Is that correct?"

Gloria promptly responded: "Yes, I..we..have. Clay caught that one immediately but did not change the facial expression.

"May I see who that choice is?" he asked.

Gloria promptly responded: "Yes..I..we..have.Clay caught that one immediately but didn't change the expression on his face.

"May I see who that choice is?" he asked

Gloria opened the 'catalog' to the page. It drew the doctor's instant approval.

"Excellent! I will tell you he is a popular choice."

Clay wondered what that meant.

"What is the next step?" Gloria asked

"Well, we will establish an appropriate date based on your cycle. We will have the frozen sperm ready at that time and simply undertake the insemination.'

"Will that be done here?"

"Yes, of course. We have complete setup"

Gloria tentatively set up an appointment as her cycle was fairly regular. When that day arrived she seemed eager to get the procedure accomplished. Clay needed to accompany her and while still annoyed with all of this, nevertheless drive her to the Clinic. When she was finished, they returned home as she was told to rest for the remainder of the day. She told him it was a simple thing and Dr Annenberg was very optimistic the procedure would result in a pregnancy. She indeed missed her next period and tested positive.

CHAPTER EIGHT

The pregnancy went as well as she had hoped. She continued to work but had arranged a two week leave of absence prior to her expected date of delivery. Both sets of parents were thrilled with all of this but as far as she knew neither was aware of the circumstances. Linda inquired frequently as to whether she as getting a new 'brothr or sister'. As it turned out, when Gloria had asked Clay if she should obtain an ultrasound prior to the delivery. He seemed indifferent so she decided they should not. She was still frustrated by Linda's seemingly slow progress and felt even more convinced d that they had made the right decision.

She had been home for ten days on her two week leave when she began to note the onset of the contractions. They were spaced far enough apart that she knew she had some time but this was certainly 'it'. She had not noted any amniotic fluid leakage, so there was no emergency but she wanted to get moving as quickly as she could. She reached for the telephone and dialed Clay using his direct line.

"Honey, I think the time has come. Can you get home real soon. I think we need to get to the hospital."

"Started, huh? OK, I really don't have anything on my schedule of importance. I'll be there as soon as I can. It's.. let's see. 2:30 so the traffic should not be too bad. Should be there in 30 minutes or so."

"Fine. I think we have some time."

Leaving his office, Clay told Laverne that it looked like Gloria was in labor and he wasn't sure when he would be back in but he would stay in contact.

"You'd better, Mr. Lawrence! Give my regards to Mrs. Lawrence and I hope all goes well."

"I will. Thanks, Laverne. Talk to you later."

Clay found himself not as much in a rush as he thought he might have been, certainly not like it was with Linda. He knew the choice of artificial insemination was molding so much of his behavior now. He did not like himself for it but it was the way it was. The drive home, as he had anticipated, was not difficult and he arrived about the time he had told Gloria. Walking in the house, he found her mildly6 but not severely uncomfortable.

"OH, honey" she exclaimed. "Thank God you're here. I think it is starting to mover along. I'd like to get going. I packed a few things"

"Fine. I'm ready. What about Linda?" 'I've talked to the nanny. She'll be here when Linda gets home. She'll stay as long as she is needed before taking any time off"

They drove towards the hospital where Linda was delivered as Gloria was using the same obstetrician who was a middle aged mam, tall with graying hair, and the distinguished look of someone who should be in charge of some medical school. He was admired by his colleagues and was popular with his patients. He did find it a little odd, in these days that they did not wish to know the sex of their child. However, he suspected that the mystery was appealing to some and he was aware that both Gloria and her husband were quite bright and accomplished.

The admission process went rather smoothly and easily, Clay thought. The obstetrics floor was painted with a rather bright hue and bland but calming etchings lining the walls. All of the rooms were private as the hospital felt this to be a necessity with expectant mothers and their husbands. There were two large windows into which a steady stream of sunlight filtered making the room quite bright and inviting.

"The contractions are coming a bit more often now, Clay"

He nodded but did not say much although he moved to hold her hand and she appreciated that She was very much aware of his apprehension and uncertainty about her choice.

The minutes inched along but finally the moment arrived. She kissed him gingerly to which he responded and told her he would be in the room. He did not want to go into the t delivery room with her although he had some so with Linda. As the day crept into night, the fading light drenched the room in a panorama of color that blended with Clay's changing thoughts and moods. How in the hell did he agree to this? How did he let her go through with it? This was just not his child and he could not get that thought out of his head. It was now an obsession. However, he did love his wife, at least he thought he still loved her but he was having difficulty understanding her desire to go through with this whole thing.

Clay passed the time with difficulty. He was concerned about her safety, of course, but even more about the consequences of what they were doing. Maybe I'm too worried about nothing. If this turns out to work, he thought, I'm sure we can have our next child together.

In the midst of his reverie, the door to the room opened and in stepped a middle –aged man still in his green scrubs.

He recognized Clay and greeted him with a degree of familiarity. "Mr. Lawrence. I'm Dr. Kline How good to see you again. Everything went fine. You have a healthy seven pound boy. Your wife is doing quite well."

Thank you so much Dr. Kline. We are both thrilled. When can I see her?"

"She will be retuned with the baby to this room for a while and then he gets to go into the newborn nursery.

She should be moved in here momentarily." All of this was accompanied by a wide senile that seemed to capsulize his acclaimed bedside manner.

As he closed the door, Clay was drawn back into that melancholy atmosphere that had floated over him like a mysterious cloud. He should be happy, he thought. Like all men, he supposed, he had always wanted a boy somewhere along the line. Now that he had one he realized that he id not really have one. It was that donor's boy and he was its custodian.

CHAPTER NINE

They named him Michael. Clay didn't know why they picked that one but it sounded good to Gloria and everyone else and he had no problem with it either. As is the usual case, the women I concentrated on his weight and length, which seemed a female staple with births. Everyone was satisfied that he was an apparent adequate size. His mother, of course, was aware of what had transpired but remained quite discrete in how she continued to interact with Gloria and her parents.

"He is a beautiful boy" Roberta had told all of them the day of the delivery. "I think I can even see some resemblance to you, Clay:" she had sheepishly added. Clay had always thought babies look just the same that soon in the cycle of their life.

"Yes, maybe" his mother had inserted ironically.

"Maybe I shouldn't bring this up but I will" Roberta said "Will you baptize him and bring him up as a Catholic?"

"Does it make a big difference to you, Roberta?" his mother asked.

"Yes and no. I know that Clay and Gloria aren't really observant in any religion and that's their choice. But, you know, family traditions and such"

"Well, I do not want religious differences entering into this marriage or affect any of the grandchildren. I know it can and maybe will here too but I hope not. Ralph, I personally don't have a problem with that. What about you?"

"Well, I thought we went through this before with Linda. The answer is the same. I have no problem."

Clay took this all in with a rather peripheral interest. It was true that they didn't seem to engage in an active religious life-style and seldom discussed it. Gloria did those things with her parents that she thought they wanted to see her do which was agreeable.

"Clay?" Gloria looked at him somewhat beseechingly.

"Fine. Fine/ whatever everyone wants. I'm fine with it."

So at the appropriate time interval, their newborn son was baptized as Michael Scott Lawrence. Clay was a bit bemused with the pomp and ceremony that surrounded this but knew it was a part of the Catholic ritual which he accepted. The presiding priest assured them that their son would have a most fulfilling life with the help of Jesus Christ. Clay wondered about that proclamation.

CHAPTER TEN

Clay gradually slipped into the role of father to Michael. It was harder than he thought it would be. He did not realize how the feeling of this being another man's child would affect him but it did. He felt that his emotional ties to him were not what they were for his daughter, even with her defects. But he seemed so much quicker than she was at every stage of development. He was surprised how Linda had taken to him. She was still his 'big sister' as she had told them more than once.

Linda had continued to be Linda. Still obviously slow but she was able to stay in the private school; where she had enrolled in kindergarten. Gloria always seemed to lean towards Michael more than Clay felt was acceptable but he remained silent. His parents had seemingly accepted the lack of any biological link to interfere with their interaction with Michael and his mother, particularly, seemed to dote over him and frequently exclaim how "cute and affectionate" he was. As time went by, it became obvious that Michael was advancing rather well, a rather marked contrast to Linda. Gloria always seemed excited when she returned from a routine visit to the pediatrician and was eager to tell Clay it seemed he was definitely above average in development, both in body size and intelligence. It was as if she was hinting to him that it seemed that 'I told you so'. He tried not to let that interfere with their relationship nor his interaction with Michael. But it was difficult not to. Not so much with him but with her. He had always felt that he and Linda's DNAs were becoming linked in that way that cements a male-female relationship. The ease of communication, the affectionate nod, the passion of the sex. Gloria continued to work. Albeit at a reduced number of hours but her status in the firm seemed well established and her income did not suffer that much. In contrast, his work, while still productive and both interesting and innovative was not as yet remunerative as was hers. That aspect, unfortunately, did add to whatever tension was still there in their relationship. However, with all that, their life went on, and while not as smoothly, at least it was not intolerable and they all seemed to settle into a rhythm that was not disagreeable

They eventually entered Michael into the same private school system as Linda's, feeling they wanted both of their children together, even with the obvious difference in intelligence. Besides, it had a good reputation and was large enough to be diversified He moved through the grades almost effortlessly and by the time he had reached the fifth grade, his teachers were indeed extolling his intellect and good manners. Linda, however, continued to plod along, needing more and more tutoring She had to repeat the third grade which was both difficult to accept. Clay had particular difficulty with this as the contrast and her brother was glowing. The apex of this seemed to be at a conference with Michael's teacher that was routine for all students. The teacher, a middle-aged plumb woman who dressed the part but seemed to wear a never ending smile couldn't use enough adjectives to describe her feelings towards him

Clay could not help but notice the smile on Gloria's face. It was more evidence for him that she was even more certain that she had made the correct decision.

"Well, thank you, Mrs. Cutter. We appreciate your kind remarks. Yes, we have noticed how very bright he seems to be."

The drive home was awkward for both. Gloria knew his underlying resentment about all of this although he had gone along without major divisiveness.

"Clay, honey. I know how this stuff bothers you and I'm sure this was more of the nail in the old coffin. I am sorry you feel this way but he is..is brilliant. I am very proud of that fact and very happy I did what I did"

As they continued to drive, Clay momentarily resumed his ruminations about why she had insisted on this and what Michael represented in the scheme of things. It indeed was an act of creating in the way available medical progress had allowed a 'custom-made' human being. Gloria did not want to take a gamble on the vagaries of Nature and seemed to desire a more' perfect' outcome for her own reproductive capabilities. She had, in a sense, become convinced that it was him that had, in some way, a defect in his genetic spermatic makeup. Not until now, at this stage of history, could this tinkering with what had been the story of mankind over the eons of time been accomplished. Cautiously, he molded his response. Basically, he still loved her or at least he thought he did. But, she was right. Hew was having trouble living with this and he guessed he showed that in various ways every day. But in that instant he realized that he either accepted the facts on the ground or. consider splitting up and he absolutely did not want that. Don't forget, he reminded himself; we still can approach the third child although Gloria had been reluctant to go ahead with that step.

"I know you are and I am too. Really. I'll get over this. Let's talk about Michael and how both of us can nurture what seems to be, as you say, some really smart kid"

"OH, honey, God, I like that, I really do. Thank you. He needs you as much as he needs me. Believe me, I do not intend to tell him that you are not his father, Period."

"I'm good with that" he answered. So it was left at that.

This modus operandi seemed to work for the next several years as Michael slowly matured and Clay settled in at his office and seemed to prosper Advancing but not in the linear fashion as Gloria, her star rising s if anointed. Was this the reason that she continually found one excurse after another not to seriously consider another child or we it still her fear of another Linda and her undying pride in Michael? She was very circuitous in their conversations about it.

Linda remainedLinda. A sweet and affectionate girl who was growing up before their eyes. She managed to barely stay even at school, but unfortunately, had to repeat the fourth grade. This only magnified the contrast with Michael.

The two children had the usual sibling conflicts that pervade this lives of the pre-adolescents. Linda, now at ten and Michael at eight, interacted in a manner that both Gloria and Clay felt was quite acceptable, given the stark difference in their cognitive ability. Therefore, it was a bit disturbing to both when one Fall night, shortly after dinner, a time that Clay attempted to be a shared experience as often as possible, Linda suddenly came out of her room crying hysterically.

"Mommy" she sobbed "Michael. He ain't nice to me"

Gloria, who frequently tried to correct some of Linda's benighted grammar, did not attempt to do so at this time.

"Honey" she answered in a bit of frustration," what in the world is wrong?"

"Michael. He hit me with a truck. I told him not to do it but he kept hitting me. I hurt"

"I'm sure he didn't mean to hurt you, dear. Boys get a little excited and rough once in a while. I've told you that."

Linda looked at her then to Clay. Even at then, she was acquiring the fearture3s that would be more prominent as she aged. She was truly a beautiful little girl, bright blue eyes that concentrated your appreciation of her beauty but now a bit dimmed with tears.

"Mommy's right, honey. Boys can get little rough. I'm sure Michael didn't mean to hurt you"

"But. I think he does hurt me, daddy. He's always trying to hit me. He's mean."

"Well, okay, Linda honey. Let us talk to him, all right?"

"Uh huih" Linda tried to stifle her crying to answer as best she could

Clay yelled for Michael to come out of his room. He did not respond.

"Michael! Did you hear me? Come here now."

When he still did not respond, Clay went to his room. Michael was sitting on his bed with his head down.

"Michael? Did you not hear me?"

He responded more quickly than Clay had anticipated.

"Well, why didn't you come out?"

I don't want to talk about that dumb cunt."

Clay was startled. He stood there speechless and began to tremble slightly. Had he heard what he thought he heard? Hearing that from any male in this household would have been disturbing but from an eight-year old? Incredulous and very. disturbing.

CHAPTER ELEVEN

"Michael. What id you just say to me?"

"She's dumb, Dad. She doesn't know what end is up. I do not like to mess around with anyone like that."

""We'll talk about that later. What I meant was the use of that word."

"What word?'

"Clay was flummoxed. Was he really talking with an eight-year old or someone much older who had mysteriously disguised himself in the body of a little boy?"

'C'mon, Mike, you know what I mean.'

"Dad, I guess you mean when I said 'cunt'"

"Yes. Who taught you that?"

"Nobody. I saw it in a novel I'm reading and found out what it meant."

"What dowe have here, Clay thought. What eight year old kid would look up that word and where did he look it up? He knew he was dealing with a smart kid but just thought but just how is this kid's IQ? And was he really 'mean'? What is this all about?"

"Well, young man. I do not want to hear that word again. Do you understand?"

"Well, OK dad. But why not? It is just a 'word"

"Yes, but it is a woodchat should be used only under special circumstances. Society has some limits on what we say at given times. Do you believe that?'

"I guess. But it is still just a word'"

Clay thought it best to simply move on to another subject. He told him that he and his mother would not tolerate physical hurt to his sister or to any other child.

"Let's go down to the den."

This time, without hesitation, Michael followed him down to the den.

"Well, young man." Gloria said "I hope your father has set you straight on a few things."

"yes, I guess sop, Mom"

"You guess?"

"I..am sure"

A undecipherable from crossed Michael's face that sent a chill up Clay's spine. He would never forget that moment and that mysterious visage would too often appear in his mind. But Michael did apologize to Linda. But the mental and to a lesser extent the physical abuse did not stop.

CHAPTER TWELVE

The years slipped by as if turning pages in a book. For most, time moves along in an inexorable orbit that leaves us clenching for each lost moment. For others, the hours seem as if stuck in mud. For Clay and Gloria, it was the rapidity of the movement that always astounded them. Michael seemed to mature too rapidly, Clay thought. His brilliance was evident to all. He was advanced two grades and now, at the age of sixteen, was a senior in high school. He remained at the same private school as Linda. Whatever it was about the school, Michael maintained a seeming sense of superiority that Clay could not ignore but about which he remained silent. Gloria thought he was smart enough to get into almost any college regardless of what secondary school he would attend so here he would stay. He had grown into a rather tall, athletic young man who was admittedly, quite handsome. He was the editor of the school newspaper, president of both his class and of the Student Council, and for the climax, the starting quarterback on the football team, even at the age of sixteen. In short: the All-American boy. Clay was both somewhat proud and a bit jealous. This, he constantly reminded himself, was not really his son. Gloria, on the other hand, exalted in his accomplishments and found many excuses to let others know how much he was accomplishing, the straight A's and his class-leading scholarship. She had told Clay more than once what indeed was the 'wonderful' choice they had made years ago. The contrast to Linda grew even more evident as they entered and progressed through their teens. Throughout, Michael continued with his abuse of Linda although now more verbal, belittling her for her 'stupidity'. Both Gloria and Clay had tried various methods to discourage him but they were not always successful. Gloria seemed less disturbed by Michael's condescension than did Clay suggesting to him that she quietly resented Linda but relished Michael's qualities.

In his senior year, Gloria, while working at her office, was informed by her secretary that the principal of Michael's school was on the phone. Strange, she felt, and a bit frightening as the school never had called her at work, only leaving messages, if need be, at their home.

"Mrs. Lawrence?"

"Yes, yes, this is Gloria Lawrence"

"Mrsd. Lawrence, this is Jim Hedly, Micheal's principal"

"Yes, of course. Mr. Hedley. We've met several times"

"Yes, I know. How are you?'

"Fine. Is there some problem?"

"Well, yes. Let me get right to the point. Michael was involved in a fight here at school. He lost his temper I gather. He got into a fight and injured another boy. This could be a serious problem.

Something about the boy being stupid. You know, Michael is such an outstanding student and leader. I could not believe this has happened but I must ask you to come to school. Now. This could end up in a legal ballyhoo and such. The boy may have a fractured jaw."

"Gloria sat as if immobilized. How could this be? Her Michael? The 'apple of her eye'.

"I don't know quite what to say, Mr. Hedley. I…really don't. I cannot believe it. Really."

"Well, as I said, neither could I. But it did happen. Please. Either you or your husband or preferably both, should come to school as soon as you can."

Thank you, Mr. Hedley. It will be taken care of."

Gloria sat glued to her chair for several minutes. Her Michael? Was this possible. She had, in fact, noticed his quick temper and his continuing battles with Linda although that seemed to be lessened now that she was in her late teens but she was still Linda. Should I call Clay about this?' No, best not. I'll go over to the school myself. Maybe get this settled and then bring him in. Or at lest I hop0e I can get this settled.'

She left her office hurriedly, telling her secretary that she had an urgent situation but she would be on her cell phone if something important needed attention. Driving quickly, too quickly she realized, to the school, a jumble of thoughts was crisscrossing her brain. As she came upon the parking area, she sat in the car for a few moments to collect those thoughts in preparation for what was to come. Why was she so panicked? Was it because this dream she had of Michael seemed so perfect. Everything she had hoped he could be. So far, he had been.

She walked through the school entrance where the familiarity was both comforting and today, disconcerting. The halls were emptied this later time in the day. Some of the teachers were still in their rooms and she recognized se4veral of them. As she opened the door to Mr. Hendley's office and walked in she noticed the entry to his office was open and glimpsing her beckoned her to come in as his secretary obviously having already left. Walking into his office, seemingly larger than she remembered, he sat behind a large oak desk with a number of mementos and photographs on its glass top.

"Mrs. Lawrence, how nice to see you, even under these circumstances. Please sit down" he directed as he swept his hand towards a chair in front of his desk. "I am so sorry to have to meet again because of Michael. He is… so representative of my ideal student that this has really surprised me and I must say, upset me as it obviously has you"

Gloria narrowed her eyes a she looked back straight into his eyes. Hedley was a man in his mid-fifties she guessed. Tall and rather handsome with an ample supply of salt and pepper hair with bright blue eyes that enhanced his demeanor. He was very popular and an effective principal as far as she knew.

"Yes" Gloria answered in a quite subdued voice, at least for her. "Is the other boy all right" she then asked, knowing this to be the appropriate first question.

"Steven? Well, as I said he might have a broken jaw and is at the emergency room as far as I know. Haven't heard anything more. Hope not. That could be a long period of recovery and eating only liquids and all that kind of bad stuff"

"What happened?"

"As far as I know, Mrs. Lawrence, they were standing in the hall, Michael, Steven and some others. Michael suddenly called him 'stupid' and Steven reacted and then the fighting began. Michael is a rather healthy young man as you know and, unfortunately, did what he did. Michael will have to tell you more."

With that, he picked up the phone and called somewhere to ask Michael to come to his office. Gloria still retained that feeling of immense pride when he walked in, even though this turn of events was a bit disturbing, Michael was now a little over six feet with flowing dark hair and piercing brown eyes. He was quite handsome. Gloria had a photo of his biological father, hidden carefully from anyone's view, and as he aged often compared their features. There was considerable resemblance and now, she wondered if Michael was ever curious as to why he did not resemble Clay in anyway physically although he did have some of her facial features. He never asked and she, of course, never discussed any of this with him. Would she ever? Clay had never pushed it so for now, it would remain buried.

Hedley gestured for him to sit on a chair on the side of his office. As he sat, he turned and gave her a riveting look that both befuddled and sent a chill ever so slightly over her. God, how strange she later thought.

"Michael, I've told your Mother about the altercation and the fact that Steven is now at the hospital with a possible broken jaw. Would you mind telling both of us what did happen to start this."

Michael, after remaining silent for a few seconds, looked first at Hedley and then back to Gloria. That strange facial expression returned. She just had never noticed it before.

"He is stupid number one and obnoxious number two"

"I'm sorry, Michael, but I don't quite understand." Hedley interjected.

"Well, Steven is one of the council members. I had asked him to do a simple task that he completely screwed up. Then, at football practice he ran the stupidest route and no way could I complete a pass to him. So, I told today that he was a stupid asshole. I guess he didn't like that"

Gloria and Hedley looked at each other and then at Michael.

"I calls them the way I sees them" Michael answered. The arrogance dripping off each word.

Gloria was baffled. She had never really heard Michael talk like this, at least not that she was party to. She knew of the incident with Linda years ago and his use of the word 'cunt' which shocked her. Since then, he seemed to be on an even keel even though he and Linda really seemed at each other's throats from time to time but there did not seem to be any physical contact between them anymore.

Hedley remained silent for a few more moments, seemingly studying this young man and trying to conflate his view of him before this incident with what he was seeing and hearing now. It didn't seem to gel. Here was this, well not 'perfect', that was never to be expected. But brilliant student, athlete, and leader and now this less than perfect provocateur. What to make of it? Not that Jekyll and Hyde shit but..really, this seemed to be awfully damn close. He could see, of course that his mother was, more than visibly shaken. It seemed as if her world was crashing. Was he her world? Why would this stun her so? He had seen other parents confronted with episodes that they did not expect or really understand but they didn't seemed to be so crushed as this woman appeared to be.

"Michael" he began "do you think you are that much smarter and better than the others?"

Michael looked at him, somewhat quizzically, as he thought about his response. Of course he was smarter and better than the 'others' whatever the fuck the 'others' meant. But he also knew he must be careful now. He had sensed, with his mother's seemingly shocked reaction to this, that he had surprised her and perhaps been a bit too cavalier in his description of the events. Slower, Michael my man, don't screw this up. People will recognize that you are smarter than they are in due time. Don't be so greedy. Tread softly.

"No, not really. I think I am smarter than Steven. Not in everything but I think in this case. Look, I'm sorry that it turned into a fight. It was my fault I guess. I should have been a bit more tolerant and thoughtful."

There, he thought, How about that for an answer. That should blow them out of the water. Need tyo get back into my groove. Stupid to let that asshole Steven provoke him into this.

He looked quickly towards Gloria. A smile seemed to be forming and her face seemed to be a bit brighter, or at least he thought so. Hedley's expression, he noted, did not seem to change. C'mon, you old fart, Michael thought; show me your good old guy stuff that everyone talks about. That answer must be what you wanted.

"Well, Mrs. Lawrence, sounds like our old Micheal, doesn't it?"

Bingo! Michael thought. Bull's eye.

"Yes, it does. So out of character, Mr. Hedley. Really it does. Don't you think she asked plaintively?

"I think so. Michael, I am glad you realized it is unnecessary, no matter what the provocation, to fight it out. Tempting, to be sure but not necessary. If you have learned that lesson, good. But the big problem is still Steven. If he has a broken jaw, you could get sued by his parents. They could ask for significant punitive action against you. It is your senior year and I'd hate to see something like this happen. You are in line to receive a number of sought after awards. I just don't know what got into you, really But."

Michael realized how dumb that fight was. Necessary, yes, but dumb in the scheme of things. He would have to be discriminating the next time he was challenged by some stupid ass like Steven.

"I know, Mr. Hedley. It was so dumb of me. Is there any way you can help me out here?"

"Yes, Mr. Hedley" Gloria interjected with a definite sense of pleading" Clay and I would be so appreciative of any help you can give..us..Michael"

Hedley thought again before answering. If that kid's jaw is broken that is trouble with a capital T. I'll not be able to stop anything then. If not, well, maybe I can get everyone together and settle this down. Michael seems like such a good kid. So goddamn smart and talented. He is in line for a top notch college. Maybe even Ivy League unless football is big for him.

"Well, we need to see how Steven is doing first. Then we'll see about the next step" was his short but considered answer.

"Is there a way of finding out now?" Gloria asked.

"Maybe. I have Mrs. Anderson's cell-phone number. She told me I could call if necessary. Perhaps it is necessary now."

Gloria was impressed with this guy. He seemed to have the situation in control and obviously liked Michael enough to go out of his way for him …and her. Yes, Michael is an impressive kid. He can do that to people. Just don't know what this crap was all about. I know he feels he is a smart and savvy kid but this? A blip, she thought. Just a blip. Was that a wink Hedley gave me? Maybe. She had obviously erased the impression that Michael had made on her with that unusual scowl at the beginning. It was real but she had chosen to ignore it.

"Mrs. Anderson? Hello, this is Jim Hedley. Hope I am not disturbing you at an inconvenient time. But it is important I know how Steven is doing."

Both Gloria and Michael stiffened and sat anxiously as he awaited her response.

"No? That is just wondeful, wonderful. Well, I was quite concerned about that [possibility. I have seen other students who did break their jaws and it was a very tough recovery time, believe me. Well, tell Steven he can certainly take a few days off from school, as I am sure the doctors already suggested that and we will be looking forward to his return. I'm sorry? Did I what?"

Gloria was relieved to hear the first part of their conversation but was uncertain what this little pasue meant.

"Have I talked to the other student yet?" Yes, yes, as a matter-of-fact, he is in here now with his Mother and feels quite badly about the whole situation and is quite happy Steven is all right. Yes, he did more or less apologize, yes he did. I'm sure he will tell Steven that in person. Yes, yes I'll be certain he understands that. Yes, you what?"

Another pause. "Well, I think that is appropriate. We don't want this incident to cause Steven or Micheal any further problems and I assume it will not. "Hedley put the receiver back in its cradle and sat for a moment before looking at Gloria and Michael again.

"They were considering taking legal action but since you seemed remorseful and he does not have a fractured jaw they are not going to pursue that. Thank goodness."

Gloria's pulse had been racing but she was starting settle down with that last announcement. They certainly did not need that legal stuff. Even though she was a competent lawyer and could have handled this with the help of her colleagues, it was obviously best to leave this alone. She was already rather defensive about Michael with Clay. Yes, he had been doing the 'fatherly;' thing that you'd expect with a teenager and seemed proud of both his academic and athletic accomplishments but...still, he was not his biological father Gloria had increasingly surmised that this was still a problem. She dearly loved Clay and that was bothersome. Maybe it's that evolutionary stuff. Men wanting to pass on their genes and all that. Well, maybe we'll try again but not now. I've thought many times about telling Michael about it but for now, I'll keep it hush-hush.

After completing the call Hedley turned to Michael.

"Well, young man, Steven is going to be all right" I insist you contact him and apologize. Hopefully, that will end this matter and we will not to take any further action. Listen, Micheal, I am willing to accept the fact that it was just one of those adolescent scenes that happens. You are just too smart to let that stuff screw you up."

Gloria again noticed that strange smile spreading over Michael's face. Why was she noticing all of this? God, this is her Michael isn't it? What the hell am I thinking about now. Forget it, Gloria, he'll be just fine.

"Don't worry, Mr. Hedley" Michael answered. "I'm good for my word. I'll be sure to talk to Steve as soon as I can and get this thing behind both of us."

"Good, very good." Hedley replied with a look of self-congratulation covering his face. "Now, Mrs. Lawrence, let us hope this is indeed behind us. I am not going to take any further disciplinary action but Michael knows there will be no more of this."

"Thank you so much, Mr. Hedley. I …still don't understand this and I will certainly do my best to guide Michael in the right direction."

"I'm sure you will. He is, as I said, too much of a prize to be wasted"

Once again, that mysterious smile traversed Micheal's face. God that irritated her. What the hell is that look?"

Meanwhile, Michael was thinking how he had pulled this off just right. God, what a load of bullshit that ol' Hedley was throwing out. 'Too much of a prize!' What a bunch of total crap!Micheal, my man, just a sample of your ability to control things. Yes, you are too smart for the rest of these stupid assholes. Maybe that even includes my good ol' mother. 'Guide me in the right direction'? What in the hell does that mean? Sounds like something out of a Victorian novel.

But he was determined to control these emotions He did appreciate his mother but not sure if he truly loved her, however. Strange. Why wouldn't he? Maybe, he thought, just because he was just too special!

Gloria thanked. Hedley as she and Michael prepared to leave his office.

"Believe me. It was my pleasure Mrs. Lawrence. You take extra care of that son of yours, understand?" he cheerfully added.

"Of course"

As they walked down the hall towards the front door of the school, she took Michael by the arm.

"Please sweetheart, don't do this stuff again. We just do not want anything to get in the way of your future, OK?"

"Of course, Mom. I really do understand. It was dumb of me to get into a fight. I'll watch it. I also don't want anything to mess up what's ahead."

She was now a bit more satisfied. However she could not get that peculiar façade he had shown in Hedley's office.

What was it? It had sent a chill through her then and still did when she thought about it again. She was persuading herself that it meant nothing. Michael was her pride and joy and still destined for greatness. She could feel it in her bones. She told him that they probably should not mention this incident to Clay. He readily agreed.

CHAPTER THIRTEEN

They never did tell Clay about the incident. As far as Gloria was concerned, Michael seemed to be back in his 'groove'. No more 'monkey business'/ at school eithr in his classes, with his friends, or his extracurricular activities. He apparently had indeed spoken to Steven and things, he had told her, were 'patched up' between them with no hard feelings. Actually, he had confronted Steven and told him not to contradict him in the future and Steven's quick assent and apparent cowering before him enhanced Michael's feeling of superiority and control over the world as he knew it. What continued to be a problem was his relationship with Linda. She was still in high school, but still at the junior level. She had managed to keep up with her peers often enough but still had been held back in the ninth grade. At eighteen, she was older than her classmates. She was now a beautiful young lady and the school boys had certainly noticed and quite frequently at that. It was apparent to all of her classmates that she was abit slow but she also was quite personable, interacting well with them as well as with her teachers. She had even tried to be a cheerleader but her motor skills were not up to the task and she gracefully abandoned the idea but received support from the other girls for effort. Michael, however, confronted her after her decision to quit.

"Well, Linda dear" he said. "Couldn't cut the cheerleading stuff, huh?"

The two of them had never developed any real relationship. He did not offer any encouragement or support and derided her even when Gloria had asked him to be more understanding and tolerant and, hopefully, helpful.

Please, Michael, I...don't want to talk to you now"

"Oh, poor little thing, couldn't handle the cheerleading test"

"Shut up!" she screamed "just leave me alone"

"Too bad. You are a real knockout. Boys would've loved seeing your little cheerleader panties as you jumped up and down"

With that, she jumped up with the obvious intention of striking him. He caught her arm.

"You fucking bitch, don't think you can hit me. You are too stupid and weak for that"

Lin da stopped in her path and now walked backwards. Suddenly, she burst out in rtears and started screaming at him.

"Get out of here, please. You are bad. So bad!"

He thought about striking her but was able to gather himself in time to avoid doing it. Wouldn't be a smart move, Michael, my man, not smart at all. He turned to retreat as Linda told him to stay out of her room.

"Look, bitch, I can come in here anytime I want. And, I would advise you not to say anything about this to Mom or Dad. I mean it, OK?"

Linda looked at him with hate in her eyes. She did not know he was her half-brother and often wondered why he turned out so smart and athletic and she.... But.But.

"Listen, Michael. It isn't good for us to hate each other. I don't like this. Please be nicer to me. I'll not tell Mom or Dad about this but....be nicer."

Michael digested what he had just heard. His mind seemed to be processing input into a cauldron almost out of his conscious control. Thinking of her words he thought, maybe, if I play this right I can have her eating out of my hand. She's probably right. No reason for me to antagonize her, She really is a dumb fucking cunt but why should I let her get in my way. He had some difficulty at times constructing a solid picture of what his way meant but he was sure it meant ultimate greatness with mass recognition of his brilliance.

"Yea. Maybe you are right, Linda. I don't really hate you. OK, let's make up" He walked over to her and gave her a quick kiss on her cheek.

Linda was uncertain how to react. She really wasn't sure why she said that or did what he did. She did not trust him, really, but she did want a better relationship with her brother. He was developing a manner of calculation and goal-setting from all that thoughts from that cauldron that was beyond his years. He maintained his decorum a t school; and continued to be recognized as an outstanding student and athlete. Gloria continued to bask in the glory that he reflected. She was more convinced that her decision to use a sperm donor was the correct one and that her particular choice could not have been better. It seemed obvious to her that combining her genes with his, both of whom she envisioned as quite superior, was paying off. She wondered why more women did not do this. God, picking the most handsome, brilliant and accomplished man should be a no-brainer. Of course, you can still have sex with your own husband and we have. He hasn't, in all of these years, brought up the idea of having more children of their own. I don't know why he hasn't but he simply hasn't. But I have been very good in bed; very good and maybe that's why he hasn't. Still, I continue on my contraceptives and I soon will be entering menopause. I am probably too old now for more children so I'll just let it lie at that.

Michael and Clay had maintained a peculiar relationship. For whatever reason or reasons, the unconscious and occasionally conscious recognition of the lack of their biological linkage, their interaction was becoming more distant and cool. While that decision of Gloria's had subsided somewhat over the years, it was a rumination that recurred and recurred.

Should he have insisted that they have another child of their own before even considering a sperm donor weighed on him. But he never brought that up tp her. A mistake? Perhaps. While he noted the apparent change, he remained suspicious of why it had occurred. Why he had suddenly become less confrontational with her was a mystery and he often scolded himself for his skepticism.

"Gloria, honey" he asked his wife one night while they were alone "have you noticed Michael's changed rapport with Linda? It seems so different Have you ever wondered why?"

"Well, I guess I apparently haven't noticed it as much as you have, but, yes, I haven't heard as much yelling between the two."

"Is that all you notice? The yelling?" he asked somewhat dismayingly

"What do you mean, all?"

"Well, honey. I know your feelings about the two of them. That's all."

Clay had never really expressed his honest take on Gloria and her son. He felt she was very much partial to Michael and often ignored Linda or tried to wash over her obvious intellectual inferiority to him. He did his best to not let this interfere with their married life. For the most part it did not. At least up to now. Sexually, they still seemed compatible but Clay had noticed a cooling from the more passionate past. Some of that, obviously, was the normal 'wear and tear' of years of marriage he suspected, but that was not all of it. Did she feel that he did not do enough with or appreciate Michael as much as she felt he should? He had never asked. Well, screw it, now, perhaps, was the time.

"Clay, please. Let's not play any fucking games. What are you talking about?" She narrowed her eyelids and seemed to scowl at him.

"C'mon, dear. You know what I mean. Michael is your darling, your hero. Your Prince Charming. You wanted a genius and well, maybe, you've got one. Linda is an albatross around your neck, isn't she?"

Gloria was actually stunned at that remark. While she knew of his resentment of her choice in the first place, she had no idea he felt quite this strongly about her relationship with Michael and Linda. She was silent for a moment, trying to assimilate what he had just said and what it all meant. Was she, in fact, that obvious in her differ4eences with the two? Had Linda really picked up on this? Did Michael? They were in their bedroom with the lamps at their bedsides on full. The shadows that played cross the ceiling seemed to be magnified and she imagined she saw Michael chasing Linda. Shit, stop this, she thought. Get Real!

"Clay, let me be as honest as I can with those accusations. Yes, I prize Michael. He is everything a mother would want in her son. And, no, Linda is not an albatross. She is a beautiful young woman now. I admire how she can carry herself under the circumstances.

Did she really believe that? Well ye. She did admire Linda's beauty. But not her intelligence. She had accepted that but would never tell Clay how she really felt, of course. What was the point? Linda was what she was, which the reason was in the first place for her to make that decision all those years ago. She probably would get through life well enough because of her beauty. And, yes, she did love her. She was still her child, actually, their child. She often wondered why Clay never asked her about having another one together. Was he too afraid of what might happen? She never asked him and again, that was that.

Clay remained pensive far longer than Gloria thought fair or reasonable. They had always enjoyed a reasonably good line of communication although she felt this was being strained. Michael? Maybe not. Perhaps just the normal passage of time and the gradual lessening of cacophony of the married state. But this did seem different. She loved Clay, truly she did. She never wanted Micheal, or Linda for that matter, to come between them. But she knew that they had. Linda was his favorite she realized. Not so much for her accomplishments but for what she was.

"Fair enough, honey" Clay answered. "I just don't want you to push Linda aside. She is very sensitive and vulnerable, as you know. Michael has been a threat to her and for some reason he has toned down that approach. I still think he has a sense of entitlement and he seems to condescend. To about everyone.

"Please. That's a bit harsh, isn't it?"

'What do you think?"

"I…"

"C'mon, Gloria. You know he feels he is some sort of superman and most of us are below his level."

"Clay! That's bullshit! I do not get the feeling he thinks of himself as some sort of superman. I really don't". But she did. She had tried to keep it out of her consciousness but it seemed to seep in, unwanted. Was that some part of his biological father's dna? She had never met him and had always felt it was best not to. But..now? Should I? The idea was intriguing. Let me find out, if I can, what kind of man he really is. Let's see if I can find him.

'I really am disturbed you feel this way, honey. I know Linda have had their run-=ins but I think he is trying to be more thoughtful. Listen, if you feel uncomfortable, tell him. Put him in his place."

Clay looked a bit incredulously at this wife. Did she really mean this? Her' hero? 'Put him in his place? That'll be the day she's comfortable with that but..who knows?

"I don't know what you mean by that. I have talked to him, many times but I'm not sure it registers"

"You think it's my job, don't you?"

He really did but he was not going there. "no, no it's both of our job. He is a terrific kid in many ways but there are some things that…well, bother me."

Gloria wasn't going to continue this conversation. She felt strongly that her decision year ago was the right one. It was obvious he and Michael were never going to be that close. Well, so be it. And, she decided she would not try to contact the biological father. Leave well enough alone.

If all of this served as a stimulus she did not hesitate to aggressively invite him to engage in sex that night which both seemed to enjoy and led Clay to believe that their relationship would endure despite all that had gone on.

At breakfast the next morning, Clay was determined to set a new course with Michael. Manufactured, yes, but necessary he felt.

"Good morning, son" he said more cheerfully than Michael had ever remembered. Suspicious, as always, he looked at him with doubt but felt a reasonable response seemed to be in order.

"Well, good morning to you, Dad. You're in rather a chipper mood today. Win the lottery? "He wanted to ask him if he had 'got some' the night before but felt better to avoid that one.

"Don't I wish. What's on your agenda today?"

"Well, a big test in calculus. Then basketball practice after school if I feel I want to play this year."

"First, how are you doing in that calculus class? I always had a bit of trouble with that one."

Michael suppressed a smile. "Well, so far looks like I'm heading for an A"

"Great. Why wouldn't you play basketball this year?"

"Well, it is my senior year and I want to get things wrapped up and ready for the next step."

"I thought you had narrowed your college c choices to one of the Ivies.

You applied to both Harvard and Yale. Isn't early acceptance coming up soon for both? And you were captain of the basketball team. I can't image your coach would let you gert away with not playing,"

"He probably wouldn't. I'm too valuable so I guess I'll go the team meeting tonight, And, yeh, I'm going to sit on those two applications. Probably get into both."

Michael's plan to be more humble and co-operative took a little hit with that statement although he did not seem to appreciate that while Clay took strong note. Jesus, he thought, the kid just thinks he is God's gift to the world. Really, he thinks he is a fucking Superman. But he was also omitted to his project of toleration.

"I'm sure you will" was his terse answer.

They sat down together for breakfast, unusal really, as Clay mostly grabbed something on the go while Michael had usually eaten already. But they shared non-entities over the coffee, cereal and toast which both had coincidentally chosen.

Gloria decided to joint hem when she heard them talking, hurrying through her make-up to be sure she could share in, what was hopefully, some sort of reconciliation.

"Hi guys' she told them cheerfully. The kitchen, large and quite bright in the morning sun, contained a nook that easily accommodated four or more and she joined them before preparing her own breakfast.

"Well, the choice seems to be cereal and toast"

"Yea, Mom" Michael told her "great minds think alike"

That sparked a chuckle amongst the three of them but Clay was more forced than spontaneous which Gloria seemed to sense. Michael, on the other hand, seemed to feel comfortable with all of this. Set things up, he told himself. Cool the whole fire scene that may have developed. Don't let either of them get in your way. Stay focused.

"Well, what has this "man talk' been all about?" she asked innocently. She was trying so hard to get these two on the same 'wave length'.

"Kind of this and that" Clay answered. Good. You know, we hardly ever have breakfast together. I love it. We really should do this more often. She sat down and joined the conversation as best she could.

"Michael was telling me he had debated whether to go to the first basketball practice tonight. I told him the team does depend on him and I don't know why there would have been any doubt"

"Not doubts" Michael slipped in ". Boredom, maybe. I like basketball but you know, after a tough football season maybe a little rest and relaxation would be welcomed. But Dad talked me out of it and yeh, I will go. I like it, don't get me wrong, and they do need me. Just a little hesitation but I'm fine"

"Great "Gloria answered. "You should be there Michael, they do depend on you. You're the captain and their best ball handler. God, I'm surprised you even gave it a thought."

Clay suspected he wanted more of that praise that he seemed to crave. The exaltation that comes from being... well, just being Michael.

Unexpectantly, Linda came down which surprised all three of them. She was chronically late in time management and to skip breakfast too frequently for Gloria's tastes but that was Linda. She too was surprised at the unusual family gathering for breakfast.

"Golly, everyone is here. Different."

"Yes, it is, sweetheart" Clay said "Nice for a change, huh?"

"Yes, it is"

Linda looked warily at Michael. Still leery of him after their encounter but had noticed she was a little more civil towards her.

"Hey, Linda lady" Michael joined in "busy day ahead?"

Clay Gloria and Linda were all stunned. Was this Michael? Clay thought: what is this 'Linda lady" stuff.

Linda proceeded to look at the three of them. She was a bit surprised by the type of question he had asked. Actually, she was. well, amazed. Looking for words, which was not always easy for her, she answered.

"Uh, yes, Michael. I am busy. I have two tests today"

Micheal knew the courses she was taking. Good ones but easy. Designed for her, he thought.

"Well, I know you'll do well"

Clay chimed in "Of course you will honey"

Actually, Linda was making it through her classes. She would graduate with her present class even though she was a bit older. Gloria was happy but couldn't find herself proud. That caused guilt but she was very clever in hiding it.

Each finished their breakfast in their own time, Linda lingering as the other three slowly left, one by one. She sat alone for a, moment or two, Gloria and Clay kissing her good-bye as was their wont. Even Michael had given her one of those quick little 'pecks' that was unexpected from him. She was comfortable with herself really. She had learned to accept her limitations but because of her beauty and personality was well accepted by most of her classmates. They knew, of course, that she was Michael's sister but no one mentioned the huge canyon between her and his intelligence. Michael was certainly recognized as the 'genius' of his class and admired for his athletic and leadership abilities. He was as handsome as Linda was beautiful and envy was not a rarity in their school. But, again, she was happy Michael did not taunt her as much anymore. Had he changed? She did not know but she remained a bit frightened of him.

CHAPTER FOURTEEN

Michael's senior year went as well as Gloria could have hoped. He captained both the basketball and football teams as was placed on the second team All-league. Clay was impressed but Michael, on the other hand, seemed to feel this was a slight and he clearly was the best quarterback in the area. Period. Clay pointed out to him that there were fifteen schools comprising the City League and second team would seemingly be a great honor. Grudgingly, Michael seemed to see the logic in that but he still remained resentful. Why can't those people, he thought, using 'those people 'as another universe it seemed, recognize just how good he was? Second team? No way. He was chosen to be the valedictorian for the May graduation, been accepted to all four of the colleges to which he had applied, all in the Ivy League. Second team? Who are they kidding?

Linda was managing the completion of her senior year in the shadow of her very accomplished brother. She had accepted the scenario. While she felt that Clay was quite supportive, it seemed that in the past two years, she had noticed her mother paying considerably more attention to Michael than to her. She had asked Clay about this one night when he had stopped in her room to check on her progress with some homework.

"Hi Honey, going OK? Anything I can help with?" He did this rather frequently, sensing the subtle neglect displayed by Gloria.

"I'm OK, Dad."

"Good. You know I'm always ready to help if I can"

"I know, Dad. You always are. But I..." her voice trailed off.

"What, Linda? But what?"

"I don't think Mom loves me"

"Linda! Why in the world would you believe that?"

"I just do."

"Of course your mother loves you. Sometimes she has trouble showing you"

"She doesn't with Michael."

Clay had been uncertain if Linda noticed what he had noticed. Obviously, she wasn't that slow. She had clearly recognized Gloria's relationship with her and with Michael. They were different. Quite different. He actually shared Linda's impressions of her mother's divided and unequal loyalty. How should he address this? Obviously better to defuse this if at all possible. He pledged himself to bring this up with Gloria. It was not good to see this potential chasm developing between them.

"You know, honey, sometimes it's that way a mother and her son. Been that way forever. You'll see when you have children of your own.

Linda looked at him with that gaze children develop to use with their parents: half-skepticism, half-admiration.

"Really?" she asked inn what seemed complete innocence. Maybe no skepticism here. Was it the fact of her innocence which was such a charming part of her personality? That and her beauty seemed to trump the 'slowness'

"Really. And you know? The same thing seems to happen between a father and daughter"

He watched with satisfaction as a smile replaced that façade of doubt. What he had just told her, both about Gloria and Michael and them was almost certainly true. But, he was still concerned about Michael. What was it that ate at him? He just did not trust him. Maybe that was just a defense against what Gloria had chosen to do all of those years ago now. Maybe it reflected how Michael came across to him. He simply was suspicious of him.

Linda came over to show her affection. He truly loved this girl. He did not love Michael

"Now, please, don't think your mother does not love you. She does"

"I know, Daddy. But not as much as you do"

He did not answer. He simply returned her hug.

That conversation troubled him. Slow as she might be but perceptive enough to recognize what he had feared she would. Should he talk to Gloria about this? While Michael had seemingly mellowed towards Linda he was uncertain if that was genuine. He left her room, however, determined to discuss this with her. It was important.

The opportunity arose sooner than he imagined. Michael had gone out with his friends and he found Gloria sitting by herself in their rather spacious living room, reading, and the television purring in the background, with her seemingly oblivious to its contents.

She looked up at him, stopping her reading as he entered.

"Hi dear. Everyhting all right with Linda?" aware that he had just left her room.

Hesitating for a few seconds seemed to ignite a look of impatience from her

"Yes and no"

"What in the hell does that mean, Clay?"

"Yes, she is basically all right and, no, some things aren't all right"

He didn't think the opportunity to explore Linda's observation would come as soon as this but, what the hell, let's just walk through this door.

"What's not right?" Gloria drove right to the point, as lawyers are wont to do.

"She doesn't think you love her as much as you love Michael"

She sat silently for a moment. Putting her book down, she seemed immobilized as she attempted to process what she had just heard.

"Nonsense "she finally responded in a manner that Clay thought was the beginning of her defense.

"Of course I love her…" she hesitated enough to signal her rationalization. "as much as I love Michael I don't know why in the world she would feel this way."

"I don't know either. But she does".

"I r4eally feel terrible that she wounds tell you that, Clay. I really do."

He decided to go for the jugular.

"C'mon, Gloria. You know what Michael means to you. He's the affirmation that you did the right thing and Linda is the living example of why you did it in the first place"

Gloria sat as if frozen. Slowly, Clay thought he was able to detect the emergence of what seemed to be a smile of sorts

"You're right, Clay. Michael is my shining example of the correct choice."

A moment of silence.

Clay remained motionless.

"And, yes, Linda was the reason I wanted to do it. You never objected that much, you really didn't"

"Would that have stopped you from going ahead?"

"Maybe. But probably not. Honey, I really do love you, I do. And I love Linda. But I admire as well as I love him. There is the difference."

"Undderstood. You know Linda has come a long way. She is well liked and, as you see, she is very beautiful."

"And I am also proud of her for that. But she isn't Michael and she never will have her brain power think he will be one of the most outstanding young men…maybe in this entire country."

The room was dimly lit, as she preferred. It seemed to outline her in rather mystical way. She also was a stunning woman. Working out at least four times a week had kept her in good health and good shape, her figure relatively unchanged since he had married her. She was also brilliant and on the cusp of becoming a senior partner in her firm He did not want this to come between them in a way that could seriously threaten their marriage. He did love and admire her. The usual things that can intrude upon a good marriage: money, sex, and in-laws did not really apply to them. But he just did not think he could get over what she had decided to do. In truth, it was belittling and rather insulting. Linda, of course, did have both of her their genes, not just his. But somehow, he felt they had screwed around with the natural order of things. Why did she think it would happen again and why did she think her donor was any better than he was? But that was not the reason she had done what she did. In the end, he felt he would have to simply come to a 'Modus Vivendi" with her. He would need to accept all of this the way it was. But he was going to make sure Gloria reassured Linda of her love from time to time in a meaningful way. He wished he had never agreed to use a surrogate sperm donor. But it was done. He could not change that. He had to quit fighting it if he wanted their marriage to continue and he did.

"I think you may be right" he told her with less than total conviction. "But can you tell her occasionally that you really do love her. She seems to have doubts although I agree she is wrong."

"C'mere you" she smiled as she beckoned him to her side. She embraced him with more passion that Clay seemed to have noticed in a while.

"Honey" she whispered as she drew closer to him. "I love you so much really do. I don't like to see you upset like this. I do love Linda but "she whispered" I am so proud of our..." she stopped in midsentence as she realized what she had just said. "Of Michael. I cannot help it. He is just such an amazing young man." She leaned over and found his lips. A rather prolonged kiss followed which seemed to arouse him a she had hoped it would. She felt his hand running over her breast.

"Ummm..sweetheart," she whispered "Enough of this crazy talk. Let's go screw'"

Laughing, they both arose from the couch and slipped into their bedroom, locking the door and spending night of what Clay considered sexual bliss.

CHAPTER FIFTEEN

It was a month before graduation. Michael, as expected, was chosen to be the valedictorian. Linda, even with her subdued residual fear of him, was still proud. Gloria was pleased to see her reaction. He had chosen to go to Harvard, one of only three from his rather large class who had been accepted at an Ivy League school. While the winter had been relatively mild, the coming of spring was still welcomed. It was a Tuesday night at the Lawrence home. Clay was at a meeting and had called to tell them he would be later than he thought. So, Gloria and the children settled in for dinner. Gloria liked that. Far too often, one or the other of them had this or that and were not always able to share the meals together even though she had tried to maneuver that throughout the year to foster closer bonds between the four of them. She felt as comfortable as she ever had with this newer relationship between Michael, Clay, and Linda. It made her work at the firm that much easier to handle. She had rose quickly there and was now one of the principals with a prominent leadership role that she carried out in a rather easily in parallel with running her household. The perfect example of the 'modern woman'

She had prepared this dinner herself which was not terribly common for her to do but she felt more 'fulfilled' in her role as a mother when she did. Michael was a bit more sophisticated in his tastes than Linda so she had decided to go 'all out' with his favorites but also acknowledging the need not to exhibit excessive favoritism towards him in her presence, would try to make the meal more 'eclectic'. She chose a caser salad with lots of anchovies for him and a light dressing for her. Chicken parmesan was the main course with asparagus tips topped with béarnaise sauce. She had stopped by her favorite bakery to obtain a chocolate mousse cake which she knew would please both of them.

The dining area was just off the kitchen. The table was glass set on a rich stainless steel foundation, reflecting Gloria's taste for uber-contemporary. The lights above were s startlingly in their modern look which was both unique and subdued and quite beautiful. The chairs were elegant and quite comfortable.;

Michael was quite cheerful that night which was pleasing to her and certainly she felt, to Linda.

"Gosh, Mom" he told her "this is some spread I must say" as he eyed the night's offerings.

"Well, thank you, Michael. I know you and Linda enjoy the parmesan. Your Dad is not a sold on it as you two. So,

I thought it would be a good thing to serve it tonight just for the three of us."

The conversation went smoothly during that dinner. Linda was more spirited than Gloria had seen for quite a while. She had not given the next step in her education much thought and Gloria and Clay had maneuvered her into considering a community college rather than a university. She had shown adequate artistic skills and had expressed an interest in design. Michael at first had chided her about this but more recently and seemingly acquiesced in their projections. Wanting to say that she was 'just too stupid' to consider much else he was able to control that impulse.

"The chicken is just swell, Mom" Linda told her in her uniquely Linda fashion.

"Well, thank you, sweetheart. You know I really do enjoy cooking. When I retire, Maybe I'll do a lot more of It.

"First of all, "Michael said, knowing you, you'll never retire. And whenever that is, Linda and I won't be here so that most likely just leaves the two of you. Bet you don't cook as much as you think when that happens."

Oh posh, Michael. I may retire sooner than you think and I'll have you know that great cooks love to cook regardless of the number involved."

O.K. O.K. you win." Michael responded with a merry attitude.

The pleasantness continued throughout the remainder of the meal and when the mousse cake was served, Linda was ecstatic.

"Oh my God, Mom. Did you get this cake at Littleton's? Linda knew her mother's favorite bakery well.

"Well, I must confess. I didn't make it and, yes, I did get it at Littleton's. Do you both not agree they have the most absolute scrumptious stuff on this planet?""

"The most absolute scrumptious stuff?" Michael agreed as he ate the cake, one of his favorites, with relish. But underneath, swirling around in his neuronal connections he was thinking how he hated these small-talk conversations with these two. One is too stupid to appreciate it and Mom, well, sometimes she is just too damn annoying. I need to do something about these two. And soon. They are going to just get in my way.

More small talk followed the meal, items of little importance to Michael but what he would consider 'vox populi'. He endured it as best he could, the impatience and annoyance seeming to gather momentum. He excused himself and went to his room where his fertile imagination introduced a scene that started to play out for him. A powerful scene that would nicely wrap up his need to do 'something' about them in a manner that he was not certain just why and how but aroused him. Why this way? He did not know but the scene just seemed to enter his mind like a preview in a movie theater Opening his door, he heard their voices still in the kitchen. Silly girl talk. Quietly he was able to pass the kitchen and get into the adjacent garage through a separate entrance. He moved to the cabinet where he found the rope he knew was there. Gathering it in his hand, he opened another cabinet where Clay had placed a rather large hunting knife that he had planned to use but never did. Good, he thought, it will serve my purpose now. His mind was racing. Many thoughts coming together in a jumble of scenarios. Tape, I need tape, he thought and found an unopened package of duct tape near the knife. Approaching the entry into the kitchen that was used by all, he left the rope to the side but took the knife and tape with him. In his frenzy he did not remember to clean off the knife handle nor think of wearing gloves. Bursting into the room, he found them both still at the table. Gloria turned around to see him standing there, knife in hand.

"Michael!" the astonishment and surprise on her face was now replaced with a terrified glance, uncertain of all of this. "Michael!...why do you have that knife? What is wrong?"

Linda jumped up and started to scream. He quickly went over to her and slapped her face and covered her mouth with his hand, holding the knife in the other.

"Shut up, you dumb cunt. Both of you shut up. One more peep and I slit her throat, understand?"

Linda was trembling, uncertain what to do. Her heart was pounding and she felt faint. Gloria sat stupefied, paralyzed by what she was seeing. She could hardly talk or move.

Finally, her head swimming, her hands wet with fearful perspiration, eyes trying hard to focus, she attempted to pull herself together and get control of this.

"Michael, honey, did …we say something, do something? What is the matter with you? I've never seen you like this before. Please, sweetheart, put that knife down before someone really gets hurt. Please don't do anything that will undo everything you've accomplished. Please."

Even as she fought hard not to lose consciousness, Linda sensed that her mother was trying to stop Michael from ruining her plans for him, not necessarily helping her. That also did not escape Michael

"Shut up! I am fucking tired of both of you"

"Michael! Why are you talking like this? What did we do?" All of this was totally incomprehensible to Gloria. Aside from that one incident with Steven and the occasional sibling go-arounds with Linda, he had never exhibited anything like this. Never.

"Nothing yet. But you will Do as I say or I swear I will cut her throat."

Gloria decided to remain as calm as she possibly could. Difficult, obviously, under these totally baffling conditions but perhaps the best approach to calming him down and defusing this without anything tragic happening.

"Fine, Michael. What….is it you want us to do?"

"Take your clothes off"

Gloria remained immobile. Uncertain of what she had just heard, she calmly asked him again.

"Michael, what is it you want?"

"You heard me. Take your fucking clothes off."

"Honey, pleased. I am your mother. I do..do not want to take my clothes off in front of you and Linda."

"Yea, well don't worry. She'll take hers off too."

Feeling Linda struggling, he held her tighter, the knife closer to her throat.

"Don't do anything foolish, Michael. Linda, relax, honey. I..don't know what's wrong really don't. This is not our Michael. Something. Someone has taken him over. God, what has happened? Your father will be home soon, son. Please, stop and we'll forget it ever happened.

"Yea, sure, bitch. Are you going to strip or do I have to rip them off of you?" She was trembling, almost uncontrollably now. How does one act one their world, a world full of pride and promise, suddenly implode? But somehow, she stood up. Trying not to fall, she slowly began to unbutton her blouse, removed it, and finding the zipper of her skirt, she pulled it down and slipped it off.

Michael eyed her. She certainly had a full figure which accelerated his frenzy. "OK, now take off your bra and panties"

""Please, Michael, do not make me do this."

"Do it!" he demanded as he pushed the blade closer to Linda.

She unhooked her bra, slipped it down her arms and slipped her panties. She now stood before him totally nude.

"Is that what you wanted, Michael? All of this just to see me naked? You could have just asked and saved yourself this stuff. That knife"

"Shut up, bitch. Stay where you are."

He pulled Linda with him to the door where he reached for the duct tape. She did not try to escape, the knife too close and Michael obviously totally out of control. Her long-standing fear of him was now horror. She became quite passive and let him put the tape over her mouth and eyes. Telling her to stay where she was, he quickly retrieved the rope, cut it to lengths to tie her hands behind her. He led her to the kitchen table and guided her to the chair where he told her to sit and not move.

Turning towards Gloria who had stood silently, too frightened and concerned to attempt to move away from this, watched him gag and tie Linda.

"Now what, Michael? Are you going to rape your mother?"

"Do you mean am I going to fuck you? Yes, I am going to fuck you, bitch"

Gloria could not believe what he was saying. She did not know whether to fight him or wait him out. When he reached out for her arm, she pulled it away.

"Leave me alone, you animal! What happened to you, Michael, what happened?' As ears started to well up, she lost complete control. As she started to sob, he struck her across her face.

"Shut up bitch! Stop your crying."

He led her to the sink. She had stopped resisting. Bending over the sink, she did not stop him from pushing her legs apart. She could not stop sobbing even when she felt him penetrating her from behind. He reached around to fondle her breasts. She was not sexually aroused but only stunned and frightened. She could not believe her sown son, her precious, brilliant, magnificent son was raping her. She did not feel him ejaculate but only his hands moving up to her throat. As she felt him starting to squeeze, she suddenly realized he was trying to choke her to death.

"No no Michael…God, stop..stop..do"

As the life began to slowly ebb, her last thoughts were poor Clay. He was right. She had defied Nature and taken a chance and lost. A monster had been created. By her.

She did not finish the sentence but dropped to the floor. He stared at her, took her arm, and felt for the pulse. There was none. A temporary sense of loss was quickly dispelled and he now turned towards Linda who, sitting in the chair, was shaking uncontrollably, her rapid breathing blending into hyperventilation. Removing his jeans and shorts, he had maintained an erection after his encounter with his mother, perspiration covering his body but still with a macabre smile on his face. Linda could only guess what had happened to her.

"Stand up, you cunt" he told her.

She had difficulty arising from the chair, her legs fighting to support her shaking body. She felt him cutting the rope that bound her hands. He left the tapes in place as she felt him tearing at her T-shirt. Swinging her around, her cut the straps of her bra. She tried moving away but he held her tightly with one hand as he unzipped her jeans and pulled them over her shoes. She felt his penis against her as he reached around to put his hand inside of her panties, rubbed her vagina and pulled them down. Removing the tape from her mouth, he pushed her down onto her knees.

"Open your fucking mouth"

She tried moving backwards but he took her head and forced it against him.

"Open your mouth or I swear I'll kill you: he shouted.

"As she slowly parted her lips, she felt his penis in her mouth. He pushed it in and out and then pulled her up, turning her around so he could enter her as he had done with Gloria.

"I bet all of your boyfriends would love to have you suck their cocks and then fuck you, huh, you little slut you."

This time he continued until he reached a climax inside of her. Satisfied, he reached up,. as he had with Gloria, towards her throat. Linda could not believe what happened next. She thought he was just going to continue doing whatever he had planned to with her when she felt his fingers tightening, she began to experience the quickening lack of air. She kicked and struggled as he relentlessly continued to compress her throat. The tape over her eyes had kept her in the dark b but now it prevented her from seeing the last light she would ever see as she slipped into unconsciousness, and then as he let her drop to the floor, she stopped breathing.

Feeling the pulseless body, he let out a strange, animal sound.

"Yes! I did it! Got rid of these damn stupid women."

He quickly left the kitchen, went up to his room and after washing himself, put his clothes back together. Finding a suitcase in his closet, he picked out several items of clothing and closed it. He moved into his mother's room and knowing where she kept her billfold, opened it to find a sizable amount of cash. Quickly descending the stairs, he crossed over the kitchen he noted the two lifeless women on the floor. No regrets or remorse. Just a grotesque feeling of satisfaction as he moved out into the adjacent garage, closed the door, climbed into his sports car and drove off into the night. A killer.

CHAPTE SIXTEEN

The night air felt quite stimulating as Clay put the keys in his car, starting it effortlessly. While Gloria had the new 'fobs' which enabled a keyless ignition, he still preferred a key in his hands and then into the ignition, the good 'old fashioned way' His Mercedes convertible was his dream car, slick and fast, crafted to his personality. His meeting had gone well. Innovative and clever, the company had expanded rapidly in the years he had been an associate and he was certain he would move up even higher on the management ladder; Well-liked and respected, he would soon approach Gloria's income level, perhaps surpass it which would give him that yearned for feeling of male respectability. Politically incorrect, machismo, perhaps, but still, he felt it. He went out of the parking garage unto the fabled streets of San Francisco. The lights of the city were gleaming as he drove purposely along the bay, marveling at the sight of the water at this time of night. The Golden

Gate Bridge loomed in the background, its lights marking the sentinel landmark, perhaps, of this beautiful city. He loved living here, glad that he had convinced Gloria to move. She had settled quite well, obviously, as had both Michael and Linda, although he suspected Michael would settle in most anywhere with his slick ability to control his life and those around him. In a way, he envied him. Too smart for his own good. Too handsome and athletic. The truly 'All-American boy'. How Gloria worshipped that kid!. Those thoughts could still cause a simmering sensation but he wanted to push those aside right now and just enjoy the ride. With the top of the car down, the wind rushed through his hair in its typical soothing but exhilarating way that Clay loved. Easy listening music was on his satellite radio, the notes flowing with the fluctuations of the rushing wind, adding to the total enjoyment of the rider and the contentment it provided.

It was almost 10PM when he finally turned the corner and pulled into his driveway. They had a three car garage, which was needed now that Michael was driving. Linda not yet given keys to her own car at her own request until she had taken a few more driving lessons. Pushing the button to open the door, he immediately noticed that Michael's car was gone. Peculiar. He did not remember that he was going to be away that night but occasional spontaneous outings were not infrequent with him. Driving his convertible into his spot next to Gloria's larger car somehow made him feel a bit inferior but he really didn't know why. There was a piece of rope sitting by the entrance to the kitchen. He was not certain he had seen that when he had left that morning. Opening the door, he was struck by the lights brilliantly illuminating the dining area amidst an eerie silence. Walking in, he was met almost immediately by the4 sight of Gloria lying nude on the floor, arranged in a fetal-like position.

The emotions that followed were a mixture of surprise, shock and disbelief

"Oh my God" he shrieked "what the hell...God".

He quickly bent over the lifeless body, and finding no pulse, shrieked again.

"She's dead! Gloria! Gloria! What.." his voice trailed off.

Trembling, he tried hard to maintain some sort of emotional control but he found that quite difficult and began shouting again "Gloria, what happened? Oh Jesus, God!".

Rising, he started to yell for Linda and Michael but as he turned himself towards the living room, he saw Linda's body by the refrigerator. He again had to steady himself as the emotions now were overpowering. Torn with fright and shock he now slid into panic. He did not want to go to Linda, suspecting what he would discover. Steadying himself, he managed to find a kitchen chair and ease himself into it before he might lose consciousness from this dose of shock. Heart pounding, hands trembling, he found it hard to focus his mind. Slowly, reason made its appearance. His panic slowly ebbed. He began to cry quietly, then louder, uncontrollably. He had not cried like this in years but he was totally devastated by what he was experiencing. Oh that this was just a bad bad dream! But it wasn't and he knew it. God, what to do? Who did this? Where is Michael? Michael? No, not...He quickly arose from the chair, avoiding looking a either Gloria or Linda's limp bodies, not even thinking now of covering tem, just dashing out of the kitchen and into the hall. The living room was dimly lit only by the automatic lamp nestled in a corner.

"Michael! Michael! Are you here? "He shouted towards the empty upstairs room.

Hoping against hope that he would answer, he quickly ascended the stairs to Michael's room. Opeing the door, it was dark, and, to his regret, empty.

Had he left before this happened? Where is he now? I'll call him on his cell phone. No, should I call 911 first? Yes, call them now. Now, Clay, call them. His mind was weaving, as if he was here but not here, gripped by fear and grief simultaneously. Nothing in his life, nothing, had prepared him for this. Standing in the midst of Michael's room, he was surrounded by the trappings of a teen-age boy, typical, but now, more foreboding than reassuring. He went to the phone next to the bed, steadying himself, to make that call. On the other end, the reassuring tones of a calmer voice.

"Yes, what is the emergency?" The voice asked.

"Yes, I just arrived at my home and" again, he needed to steady himself and answer in a coherent manner. This was important.

"I found my wife and daughter. Someone…." voice trailing, grasping to return to reality, "Someone has…. I think… killed them."

Those words. Those awful words that he would never forget. They seared his brain like a Bunsen burner, igniting an ocean of emotions once again.

A brief moment of silence on the other end. Then: "yes, sir. Did you say you think they are dead?"

"Yes"

"Stay where you are, sir. Do not touch anything if you can avoid it. The police will be there soon. What is your address?"

Clay quickly gave her the street and number. She again told him to stay where he was and try not to disturb anything. Did he understand?

"Yes, I understand. Please hurry, I…."

"We will. Just stay as calm as you can"

Clay suspected that was the usual admonition: "Stay Calm ". But the meaning of that word lost all of its context in this setting.

He did not want to return to the kitchen area. Did not want to see those images again. Descending the stairs, he held onto the bannister railing and turned into the living room area. Turning on a soft light, he found his favorite chair. Time has a strange way of affecting us, he thought. This wait was agaonioz9nfg, each second beating like a moment of eternity, with no end in sight. He was completely rudderless at this point, swimming in a sea of fear, uncertainty, and utter despair. Was this real? How could such a thing happen? To both of them? To both of them! Once again, he wanted to hear an alarm clock, awakening him from a horrible dream but he really knew that was just a fantasy. This had happened it was happening and he did not know how he could possibly deal with it. What seemed a perfectly normal life ended? Just like that? Why? And, Michael, His thoughts continued to focus on Michael. Where was he? He did not want to entertain the possibility that he was involved in this. That would be just too catastrophic. But now, in the distance and jolting him back into reality, came the enlarging volume of a siren. Why did they need to use a siren? He tensed as the sound closed in and just stopped. How many times had he heard a siren in his life? Hundreds? But this siren was in a class by itself. The familiar ring of the doorbell aroused him from his semi-reverie and he rose to open the door. Standing before him were two burly policeman. One seemed to be in his fifties and the other much younger. Both projected authority, their faces grim but not threatening.

"Mr. Lawrence?"

"Yes"

"What happened here? May we come in so we can help you?"

He felt dazed and forgetful. Of course they should come in.

"Yes of course. Please step in officers"

He led them, hesitantly, carefully, into the kitchen. They glanced at him with a look that Clay perceived as both empathy and suspicion. But he had been careful and not reentered that scene nor touched anything in the area. Their bodies lay as he had found them.

"Mr. Lawrence, we will need to rope this area off and call in our detectives. They will need to question you and get started on helping you solve this horrible tragedy. We can cover the bodies if you like. I'm sure this is difficult for you."

"Yes, very difficult" Thank you. I would appreciate that."

The younger man went out and returned with two blankets that he used to cover both Gloria and Linda. The simple act of removing them from sight was therapeutic for him. He was able to relax a bit, the warmth returning to his hands and the saliva to his mouth. There was small talk between him and the two officers as they roped off the area and went outside to place that gaudy yellow strip around the front of the house that would tell the neighborhood something awful might have taken place close to them. Actually, his home was a bit secluded. But still.

Fortunately, two detectives arrived within half an hour of the call for them. Both were dressed in suits with crisp white shirts and ties that seemed to match appropriately. Not the stereotype of the ruffled 'cop' in his disheveled attire. But why that impressed him was uncertain but it did seem to lead to a sense of expertise and trust emanating from that appearance. The older man introduced himself as Karl, the younger as Terry. Voices soft, their approach comforting, which seemed to indicate to Clay that he was not under any suspicion but he knew he would be, of course. They walked him though his evening, taking notes as to where he had been and with whom. Fortunately, he had not been alone, the meeting having taken place at a familiar Italian restaurant followed by a presentation by one of the new young employees. A pleasant night that now seemed centuries ago, his past life a memory, the horror of this overwhelming everything.

"And you have a son?"

"Yes. Michael. Michael is our..son"

"How old is he"? The older one named Karl asked in a very businesslike manner. Old stuff to these guys Clay guessed. Old stuff.

"Eighteen"

"Any problems with him? Anything we need to know?"

Clay knew, somewhat instinctively, that he should not hesitate with his answer.

"Not really. He is a very accomplished young man. Straight A student, valedictorian, big time athlete, all of that stuff."

Eyeing him carefully, perhaps to note his facial expression with that answer, still unsmiling, Karl told him that was a very impressive résumé.

"And at home. Any problems with your wife or daughter?"

He knew that he would have trouble with that question but, again, tried to maintain the maximum self-control.

"Gloria. His mother. Adored and idolized him. Absolutely idolized him"

"And you?"

"I was very impressed with his accomplishments."

The younger detective now joined the interrogation.

"But you did not idolize him?"

"Well, no, I can't say I idolize him but I am certainly proud."

Uncertain if that was the answer he should have given, Clay simply stopped saying anything more until questioned He felt he should bring out the problems with Michael and Linda had encountered but as far as he knew, that had been resolved and they seemingly were cordial to one another.

"How did he and your daughter get along? Any problem there?"

"The usual sibling stuff. Nothing more."

There probably was but Clay did not know how to phrase that nor if it really had any bearing on what had happened. But he did wonder.

"Where is he know?"

"I..I really don't know. I went into his room. He is gone and so is his car."

"Did he leave any messages as to where he was going?"

"No..no, come to think of it. I did not see any notes in his room or...anywhere else in the house."

"Do you think he left, then, before this all took place?"

Clay felt as if he was now in another world, divorced from reality. What were they driving at? My God, do they think Michael did this?

"I don't know." That is all he could say. Depressed, frightened, and confused all at the same time, he did not know what more to tell them. His wife and beautiful daughter were both dead and Michael, her son, was not here.

As they exchanged eye contact with one another, Clay thought he was receiving a feeling of a growing suspicion of Michael. He waited for their next question or their response.

The one who was named Karl, balding with a bit of gray infiltrating but also a very sturdy frame that seemed to convey hidden power, asked Clay the model of Michael's car and where he thought he could be at this hour.

"He has a used Chevrolet Camaro. Again, Officer, I just don't know where he could be at this time of night. He should be home anytime now I suspect."

Clay glanced at the large clock on the kitchen wall, one of Gloria's proud accoutrements that showed the time of the world for everyone, she had said.

Karl nodded at Clay as he, too, looked at that clock, watching it a bit longer than one would expect, perhaps waiting for it to tell him what the next minute might bring.

They went about their business for another half an hour, checking the scene while awaiting the representative of the coroner's office. The two uniformed officers came into tell them Harold was on his way. Shortly, a tall rather young man entered.

"Hey, Harold" Terry welcomed him.

"Guys. What's going on?" he asked rather nonchalantly.

"Harold, this is Clay Lawrence. He came back from a meeting earlier and found his wife and daughter on the floor.

Terry then proceeded to give him the information they had so far gathered. He then walked over to where Gloria's body lay, removed the blanket and briefly checked a few details. Repeating the same maneuvers with Linda, he replaced the blankets and returned to where the three of them were sitting.

"Well, we'll have to do more down at the morgue but I didn't see any gunshot wounds or evidence of stabbing. Rather obvious marks on both of their throats so we would have to guess whoever did this strangled both of them to death don't know if there was any sexual assault. Have to check that out later of course. Please continue to use the rubber gloves as we'll need fingerprints etcetera"

"Of course" Karl responded." Mr. Lawrence, we will check out your meeting tonight. Don't be alarmed> While you, of course, have to be a suspect at this time, if everything rings true, there is no problem. Your son, unfortunately, must also be a suspect. We will need the license plate number so we can put out a bulletin on him if you cannot contact him or if he doesn't return within an hour or two. It is close to midnight"

"I understand d. Do I need to come with you?"

"No, not really. You agree, Terry?"

"Yes, we'll keep in close touch"

They removed both bodies from the kitchen, loading them into an ambulance that had accompanied the coroner's aide, leaving Clay by himself, now more isolated and utterly despondent. He cried quietly as he sat in the kitchen where just a short time ago they had all shared what seemed a happy breakfast. His mind was awhirl now, trying to crowd out the memories of both Gloria and Linda. Both gone. Who in the hell did this goddamn awful thing. Could it rally be Michael? Was he actually capable of doing something like this? This All-American boy? This Adonis? And then he thought that Gloria had chosen to do this. To use another man's sperm to create what she thought was the realization of her dreams, to avoid again, an 'accident' that was Linda. They never did meet the donor, didn't k now any more than what that piece of paper told them. Was there something that they really did not know? Some skeleton in the proverbial closet that been hidden? And where was Michael? He would call his cell phone again. He had to try to something now, anything but just sit here in this empty house, now occupied by those ghosts he did not want to meet. Dialing the number, he waited with both impatience and trepidation for him to answer. But he did not.

CHAPTER SEVENTEEN

It was a fitful night. Sleep really did not come as his mind leapt from one thought to the other: images of Gloria and Linda when they were alive and how he had found them last night, disbelief that she was not lying next to him, and the image of Michael, burning in his brain with the winds of anger blowing with more ferocity. Unable to sleep, he went down to the living room, turned on a light, and simply stared at the walls as if they could remind him of the good times and give him some succor. But they did not. Drifting in time, he unexpectedly fell into a deeper sleep then he imagined possible only to be suddenly awakened by the ring of the phone. Glancing at a nearby clock, it was 7:30, the sun just gaining its momentum and filtering into the room blocking out the dark of the night as he reached for the phone.

"Hello" he answered innocently, not certain what to hear.

"Mr. Lawrence" came the response.

"Yes"

"Mr. Lawrence, this is detective Crowley, Karl Crowley. We met last night."

Trying to clear his head from the confusion, he instinctively answered: "Yes, of course. What is it?"

"Well, I wanted to give you our report as it stands as of now. They were both sexually assaulted and strangled to death. The coroner figures the incident occurred about 7:30 last night. We do have DNA material, which, of course, will be extremely helpful. We will need a sample from you and your son. Routine, you understand, but necessary."

"Yes, yes, of course. I need to be at the..I guess at the San Mateo..police headquarters?"

"Yes, at the San Mateo office. Anytime today before 4:30 would be fine. Mr. Lawrence, just ask for the coroner's office and they will know why you are there. Has your son been home yet? We will most definitely need him too."

Uncertain if Michael had slipped in while he had so fitfully caught some sleep, Clay needed to check his room to answer the detective.

"Fine. I'll hold on while you check."

His heart racing, Clay quickly ascended the stairs to Michael's room. He did not know what he wanted to see. Why that was the case was a bit mysterious. Opening the door, he quickly scanned the room and, to either his disappointment or surprise, found it empty. Unchanged since last night. Pic king up the phone in the room, hesitating a bit, he answered Crowley

"Detective, he is not in his room. I don't think he came in at all last night. I have no idea where he is.

"Is that unusual? His not coming home at all during the night?"

"Without us knowing where he plans to be? Yes, very unusual. I'd say that has not happened before" as far as I know."

"Well, Mr. Lawrence. Sorry to say this but it certainly is more definite about placing your son on our list of suspects. We will certainly put out an all-points bulletin. Is his license under his name?"

"Yes"

"Any change in cars since he last registered?"

"No"

"We can get all of the information that we will need from our records. But, we do need a sample of his DNA. Not much. Would you be able to find a toothbrush he his recently used? We might be able get a sample off of that although that may be tricky depending on the time interval from when he last used it."

"I think I can find his toothbrush if he did not take it with him, wherever he went."

"If so, bring it with you when you come in later today. And wrap it in cellophane if you have any around or aluminum paper if not"

Yes..yes, detective, I will. I still cannot believe this has happened. I just cannot. And, Michael. He. I'll be in later."

"I am very sorry about your loss. I truly am. Let me know if there is anything I can do. Obviously, we will be in touch with you. How are you holding up?"

"Jesus, not well. Not well. My wife, my daughter. Raped? Murdered. But thank you, detective. I do appreciate your concern."

He knew the DNA would be, while not conclusive, obviously helpful. Could they really get enough from?

Michael's toothbrush? Apparently so according to Crowley. Going into his bathroom, he was struck by the neatness of the place, the warmth that seemed inappropriate now. Spying the toothbrush stand, he quickly picked up one that was still in it place. He carried it to the kitchen, wrapped it in cellophane, and put in a box he found. It was quite bright now, the sunlight streaming into the kitchen seemingly seeking to erase the nightmarish residue that was last night, s if it never occurred. But it did not. Fighting hard not to relive the vision of those two bodies, two beautiful women, his prides and joy, gone. Gone. Countless other times had seen him sympathizing with those who had lost a loved one, naturally or not so naturally. You can empathize but one can never, never have this feeling when it actually happened to you. To you!

Knowing he had to get himself together and organize his next moves, he moved to his favorite chair in the living room. Ordinarily a source of comfort and serenity, it was not that now regretfully. First and foremost, of course, would be to get to the San Mateo station with his and Michael's DNA. But he suddenly realized that funeral arrangements would have to be made. He had not yet contacted either his or Gloria's parents. Had the San Francisco Chronicle arrived yet? Almost certainly it had but he was so out of sync that he had not, as was his routine, gone to pick it from the drive and enjoy what he could while at breakfast. He assumed the story had not yet appeared as no one had called and, strangely, may not have been on the late television newscast or if so, no one had seemingly watched it.

It was now just past eight. Surely, someone had seen the news about this. Where were the calls? But he felt he must call Gloria's parents. They might not yet have heard in St. Cloud. It was ten in the morning there. This was going to very, very difficult. He wished he could do this in person but, of course, that would be impossible, given the circumstances and the distance. But he had to do it. Now. Before they heard it from someone else. And they would, given the time differences. Gloria always did the calling but he made it a point to speak with them when she did but, now, unfortunately, he did not know their number. Assuming it was in that little directory she kept in the kitchen, he again went into that forbidding and now, foreboding place to retrieve it. Last in San Francisco four months ago, they were always seemingly happy to see the 'nice family' situation and very proud, of course, of Michael but also quite tolerant and loving of Linda. Finding the number, he lifted the phone but then put it back in its cradle, unable to gather enough courage to make that call.

C'mon, Clay, he told himself, you must do this. You owe it to Gloria and Linda.

Again, he picked up the phone, this time with a little more confidence but still very apprehensive, but not unexpected under the circumstances. Who wouldn't be? Telling a parent that their daughter is dead? Murdered for Christ's sake. He would not tell them she had been sexually assaulted. No way. Enough misery at one time. Dialing, he felt his chest thumping, a cool wetness in his palms, sure signs of anxiety, expected, but unwelcomed.

One, two, three rings. Were they not at home? This was a weekday and he couldn't be sure they were but on the third ring, the familiar voice of his mother –in-law, Roberta Pausing, taking his time, trying to steady himself, he began: "Roberta, I …have some terrible news for you."

"Clay, what are you talking about? What bad news? Is everyone all right?"

Good. She had not heard yet. It would have to come from him. A miserable task but at least from him. But how to answer that? How do you tell a parent who has lost their child? He did and he was finding it almost impossible to deal with it.

"Bobbie, Bobbie"...his vice dropped off, he held the phone down by his die, tears again flowing down his face, hoping they would erase all of this,. But they would not. So talk to her.

"Gloria. She was. Oh God, Bobbie, she was....murdered last night"

Silence. Complete silence. Then, a shriek the nature of which Clay had never heard before. It flowed over him like a crashing wave, a bolt of lightning ripping into his heart.

"Clay" she said finally after composing herself. "You cannot mean this. Gloria was murdered? B y whom? How? Oh my God, Clay. I..." then a complete breakdown, the screams and cries weaving together in a horrible cacophony of agony and disbelief, of rejection, and total, complete horror.

When they both had gathered their emotions enough to continue the conversation, Clay told her, as honestly she could, what he had found the night before. As she heard that Linda had suffered the same fate, the screams started again. She did not answer for some time. Clay worried that she had fainted and finally, shouting into the phone, he became desperate.

Wishing he could have told her in person, he was confused about the next step. Where was George? Was he in the house? Where? Finally, a voice on the other end.

"I'm sorry, Clay." The voice replied. Broken and signifying her bewilderment and horror. "I don't know what to say. We will be out there immediately. I don't know how I can tell this to George but I will have to. She was his pride and joy. Michael. How is he?"

Clay hesitated, confused, still uncertain how to answer that question.

"I haven't been able to find him. He was out last night when I came home. But I assume he is all right." He did not go further. Too much at one time.

"Thank God for that. Please call me when you talk to him. I want to be sure he is all right. He will be devastated by this. Devastated."

"Yes...I certainly will. Let me know the time you will be arriving."

"As soon as we can make the arrangements. Oh God, Clay, I don't know how we will be able to come to your home. But. We will see you soon"

As he hung up the phone Clay was immobilized by her comment. Devastated? Was he devastated or the devastator? Growing more suspicious by the minute, his thoughts were interrupted by the jarring high-pitched ring of the telephone. Looking at the identifying name, it was his mother. Well, he thought the other piece of the miserable necessities surrounding this goddamn nightmare.

"Clay! Clay! "She literally screamed into the phone. "My God, Clay, what. I have been in a state of shock since I heard. Why didn't you call me earlier?"

"Mom, believe me, so much. so much has been going on..I"

"Yes, Okay. But..I am coming over now."

He knew she was not to be restrained and he offered no resistance. Perhaps she could help him with the funeral arrangements, a prospect he found quite disturbing. But for now? To the police station, ultimately. If that DNA matched? Before he could ponder that possibility further, the ringing of that phone started. Noting the names on the answering machine, there were none he wished to speak to at this point. He did not answer but let the machine record the messages: sad ones, surprised ones, terrified ones, sympathetic ones. From his office, from hers, from friends and neighbors. The word was certainly out. He just hoped none would come over to the house unannounced, their presence symbolizing some sort of collective neighborly grief that he just wasn't yet able to face. When the doorbell rang, he gingerly opened the curtains that he had purposely drawn and saw his mother and father standing on the porch. Quickly moving to let them in, his mother fairly fell into his arms.

"Oh Jesus, Clay. I am so sorry. And terrified. Who..what happened? Pleased tell us."

Her tears dropped onto his shirt, her arms tightly held around him in a loving bear-hug. He had always had a wonderfully warm relationship with her and even now, especially now, providing that maternal comfort that he needed.

He was more surprised when his father, usually emotionally distanced but still attentive and seldom dismissive, moved to embrace him simultaneously, his arms wrapped around him and his mother.

"Never, never in my life" he said in a broken rhythm camouflaging his obvious distress "would I have expected anything like this."

"Neither would I have, Dad" Clay answered now that the necessary but destabilizing meeting had ended. He went on to describe what he had encountered upon his return last night, the description given in what still seemed to him a horrible dream.

"God, I cannot imagine how you felt when you found them" Talking through a curtain of tears, his mother was still unbelieving that they were even at this place at this time talking about such a thing. Such a thing!

"I cannot describe it. Just goddamn horror, that's what it was. Goddamn horrible! "Those words flowed over his parents like a torrent of hell-driven fire, emphasizing to them what they expected: the depth of his feelings.

"Clay, Honey. "His mother continued "I know this isn't.. maybe it is, I don't know, but what about the..fun.."

"The funeral" Clay interrupted." I have given it a bit of thought. I know it has to be done but..i just want to find out who is responsible for this stuff. Soon. So I can put my hands around his throat and."

She cut him off with a stout, parenteral command: "Stop Clay. Please, I know..how you must feel even though I just cannot get my feelings stitched together here. But, please don't make matters even worse. Let the police handle this. Promise?"

Why he felt uncertain as to how to answer he was not sure. Would he really choke the person who had been discovered to have committed these atrocities against him? What if, indeed it was Michael? What if? But for now.

"Yes, Mom. I'm sorry. I am so screwed up now that sometimes I cannot think straight." With that, he felt the tears coming again. This just did not seem to be in his nature. These tears? This...crying. But on they came, flowing over his cheeks in a small but detectable stream. Wanting to avoid another exhibition of his emotional instability and grief at this particular moment, he tensed up and tried to move on to his Mother's inquiry about the funerals.

He and his parents then began the very difficult assignment of planning for a double funeral. His father said he would take over and get it done as he knew this was going to be too hard for his son to do. Clay felt quite appreciative of course. While his relationship with his father was not really close in the true sense of the word, he had always found him to be supportive and helpful. And wise in a non-intellectual but practical and effective manner. He sat there while they discussed the possible arrangements, his mind still in a bit of a fog. Neither Carole or George were religious, Clay knew that. But there was an uncertainty about a Catholic funeral. They obviously needed to communicate with Gloria's family. Clay told them they should contact them now as they will be planning to come here as soon as possible.

"Of course, Clay "George replied "we will call now and hope they are not incommunicado"

They did make the connection. The conversation between his mother and Bobbie was a difficult one and Clay cringed at the emotions that it evoked. But, it was decided that yes, Bobbie would prefer a Mass at a Catholic church, if possible. But if that was not possible, she suggested that a priest conduct the funeral wherever it was held. A compromise, to be sure, but that seemed to satisfy her.

So, Carole and George assumed the roles of facilitators, surprising Clay with their efficiency and determination in this trying time. He stood back as if observing the scene from another world as the plans were finalized to use a memorial chapel with a priest presiding. The time was set for two days to give Gloria's family, both from Minnesota and various areas scattered throughout the country and elsewhere to get to San Francisco. But he still needed to get that toothbrush to the police lab as soon as possible. His rage, blanketed now by uncertainty, might erupt with the appropriate confirmation and he somehow realized that. If it was Michael. If.

"Honey" she turned forlornly towards him. "You seem in a hurry about something. What is it?"

"Something I must do at the police station. Mom. Nothing big but I need to get it done today. I know you and Dad are miserable and…let me get that done. I want to come over tonight for…if you can. Any kind of dinner in your own way."

It was a plaintive request. A return to the womb, if you will, and he realized that his mother's cooking was, had been, outstanding and for some reason he found solace in the thought of eating again with them. This time, though, alone.

Again, she embraced him, trembling yet transmitting that current that flows from mother to child. It seems to say: 'I will help you. No matter what.'

"Oh yes, sweetheart. That is the least I can do for you. You need to do what you need to do. Dad and I will finish up here. I..I do hope you can get in touch with Michael. I just do not understand where he is. I really don't. You're sure he didn't go to school?"

"Yes, Mom. I checked. He is not there."

"Well..I'll have your favorite ready for you tonight. I promise. What time is good for you.?"

Let's say seven."

"Fine"

With that, Clay kissed her again and gave his father another hug, still disbelieving he was experiencing this much emotion from him."

And for the first time since his return to find that indescribable scene of horror, he walked out of the house to his car, toothbrush in hand and a new sense of determination. He was going to find who destroyed his life if it was the last thing he would do.

CHAPTER EIGHTEEN

Arriving at the police headquarters, he was quickly directed to the laboratory area where the toothbrush was transferred for the DNA testing. Karl had told him that there were adequate material from the crime scene for any DNA match purposes and he was informed that he would be notified as soon as the work was done. Within twenty-four hours he was assured and so he gave them, once again his cell phone number and left the building with a panoply of emotions: anger, disbelief, and continued profound grief. He just could not come to grips with the gruesome ending of their lives. Strangely he was ab le to recognize that no one would have an easy time with this and how long it would take him was a depressing thought. And Michael, Michael. Nothing from him. Nothing. News of the tragedy was all over the media by now and certainly he would have heard of it. And, even if he hadn't, Clay had not heard anything from him and he still was not answering his cell phone. His suspicion continued to mount and he now was more convinced that Michael was, in some way, involved in what had transpired in that kitchen.

San Mateo was beautiful, this part of California was beautiful. The mountain ranges in the distance, the rolling ocean nearby with the ever present blueness above painted a picture of utter tranquility. But not now. Not for him, at least. Even as he drove the winding roads, he knew nothing would ever be the same. He had not even started to answer the calls that were coming in on his phones. The world knew now of the murders. Yes, that was the word. The murders. Not singular. Plural. But they could wait. As he drove, he decided to duck into a nearby coffee shop he frequented fairly often. While not exactly removed from the madding crowd, it might, at least, it had offered that sense of relaxation and escape from the work world that he had welcomed. Tucked away in a small shopping center, the coffee shop with its familiar mermaid logo, seemed especially welcomed. It was mid-afternoon and there were a number of empty seats, a rarity at this location. He ordered his usual: strong, pungent coffee, steaming hot to which he added a non-caloric sweeteners and a touch of cream. Perfect. It seemed, now, as if he was sitting down to a gourmet meal but with only that cup of coffee.

He chose an outdoor table with the view of the mountains. Drifting into thought, it seemed as if it was the first time that he could think somewhat coherently. What was it, if it indeed was Michael that drove him to do such a terrible thing? There were few specific signs that this was coming, aside from his continued confrontations with Linda, which he could dismiss as not a rare sibling occurrence. He, of course, often exhibited a sense of superiority and condescension but he was that good in so many things that Clay had dismissed this as just the manifestation of an enlarging ego. But something in his...DNA..went wrong. DNA? Yes, DNA. Goddamn, I cannot forgot that half of him came from that...Adonis she picked. What if... if other women had chosen him? If so, and they had sons, what became of them? What became of the donor himself? Clay always worried if you screw around with Nature, sometimes it comes back to bite you. What was that movement that was popular in the 20's? Eugenics? Yea, it was Eugenics. Nutty as hell but a lot of people bought into it, including, it seems the Nazis. Whoa, Clay. You still haven't heard about the DNA match or no match. But, if it does. Well, that will lead to checking some of this stuff out. That of course, along with finding Michael. If it matches. Just hold your horses, pal. Take your time. Enjoy the coffee now. Enjoy. Yea, sure, Enjoy. For now, he knew he needed to contact his office. He was certain they were aware of what happended.He was going to request an indefinite leave of absence so he could sort all of this out. Dialing the familiar number, he tried to remember how it was just a few days ago. It might as well have been a century. How one's life can change so abruptly! Nothing profound about that but when it hits home, profundity is an understatement. As they had not yet moved to a computerized answering system, Clay felt a sense of familiarity and peace, actually, when the very feminine voice answered.

"Jeannine. This is Clay Lawrence. May I please speak to Kyle? ".

There was a pause and then, expectedly, the outpouring he knew was coming.

"Mr. Lawrence. Thank God. We all have been frantic here since all that...that terrible news. And when you did not answer your phone, we."

"Yes, thank you Jeannine. I'm sorry about that. Just too much right now and I was delinquent about answering all the calls."

"Are you all right?"

"As best as can be expected."

"If there is anything I or anyone can do to help, please let us know. Hold on, Mr. Carey will be anxious to hear from you"

Clay waited, somewhat anxiously, for the BIG MAN to answer the call. Kyle Carey was a very bright and aggressive guy but honest and forthcoming. He had built the company almost from scratch, albeit a bit of help from his father. Damn good job, too.

Then the familiar, deep, self-confident voice of Kyle Carey.

"Jesus, man, what the fuck is going on? Your wife and daughter! I..none of us can believe this, really. Tell me what I can do."

"Yeh. It is ...indescribable, Kyle. Indescribable. Murdered. That.." he started to break down somewhat, something he did not want to do but all of this starting to its expected emotional toll on him. "Anyway, the cops are all over this. Hope to have some answers soon so we can get the son-of-a-bitch who did it. But, I need some time off. I know there are…"

Kyle quickly interrupted him.

"Listen, man. You take all the time you need. Seriously. We can handle anything. Just find who was responsible. And, Clay, you know your job is very secure and we will help in any way we can"

"Thanks, Kyle. As the old saying goes, I needed that."

While that did not surprise him, he was admittedly pleased that Kyle was so accommodating. Wasn't quite like him, really. But knowing your position is in no jeopardy is always reassuring. As he started to sip the coffee, having allowed it to cool a bit, his cell phone gave that familiar ring and when he saw it was Karl, he quickly tapped the answering icon with the slightest trembling of his hand.

"Hello. Clay Lawrence here."

"Mr. Lawrence. Hello, Karl Crowley. We have matched the DNA. It definitely is Michael's"

Clay was not shocked but was still in some degree of disbelief, Michael, Michael, you son-of-a bitch, you killed them both.

"Mr. Lawrence? Are you all right? Are you there?"

"Yes, yes, detective. I'm sorry. That came as a…shock." It didn't but he felt that was the appropriate response.

"I can understand. Listen, we will get an all-points bulletin out for his apprehension. We are going to charge him with two counts of murder. Do you understand? Please, Mr. Lawrence, let us do the police work. Don't be a vigilante here."

"Yes, of course. You can count on me to help in any way I can."

"Good. Believe me, I am personally going to take charge of this one. Vicious sort of thing what he did. To his mother and sister, yet. Hideous."

"Thank you. Is there anything you need me for at this point?"

"Yes. If you can drop by tomorrow at your convenience and perhaps give us some info on him that we might turn up. Traits, peccadilloes. That sort of thing."

"Yes, of course. I'll try to get in to see you in the morning."

"Fine. I will plan to be in my office all morning. So just check in and I'll try to see you immediately. Mr. Lawrence, I am so sorry. But we will apprehend him, I promise you."

With that, Clay ended the call. He sat for what seemed an eternity although his coffee was still warm when he took the next sip.

Michael, he thought, it was you. Well, detective, I know you will do your best. But first, I need to find out more about that…that DNA. And, I swear I am going to get him. Myself. Get that bastard.

But. First things first. Tonight he would go to his mother's as planned. Surprisingly, he was looking forward to her cooking. She was a terrific cook and even in this state of misery, some part of his brain took him back to his childhood with all the calming balm that often provides. So, he left that serene surroundings, back into his car, and the drive to their home. Yes, also, to see what plans had been made for the funerals. For what would certainly be the most miserable day of his life.

CHAPTER NINETEEN

His parents' home was not where he grew up but retained much of the same warm atmosphere that he mother was always able to create. Anywhere. It did not bring him peace but it did bring him back to that era when, as a boy, he had the concerns that always seem trivial in retrospect to all of us. But they were those times that, if unencumbered by ill fortune, can rekindle that nostalgia that is soothing and welcomed. She had prepared the meal that she had prepared that night he came to seek their consul concerning Gloria's decision to use a sperm bank to create what she hoped would be her 'Superman'. Some Superman! Now he had to tell them of the DNA match. How would they take that? But it had to be done. He decided to wait until after the meal was completed, to make it as comfortable as he could under the circumstances. His mother had taken great pains to dot the I's and cross the t's on the food to make it 'special' for him.

No reason to spoil that just yet. But he would have to tell them.

"God, Mom, you don't know how damn good this stuff tastes."

"Thank you, Clayton. I hope…I hope it gives you a bit of solace after this horrible day. By the way, we have talked to Bobbie and George. They want, if we agreed, to hold the funerals in a chapel of our choice but with a Catholic priest presiding. I went ahead and contacted that chapel not far from your home and made the arrangement with the diocese to provide a priest. I know Gloria seldom went to Church or confession but, she is Catholic, and that is what her parents want. I assumed you would have no problems with any of that."

Clay was trying to absorb all of that. They weren't rally talking about his wife and daughter were they? Yes, they were.

"No, no, of course not, Mom. Thank you. Thank you both for taking that burden off my shoulders"

"Oh, please, honey. That's the least we could do."

"When is the funeral?"

"Friday. That gives everyone the time to get here."

Two days, Clay thought. Two days of dread. But he would sue the time to formulate his plans. This saga is just beginning, he thought. Would they apprehend Michael first? Well, nothing he could do about that possibility.

At that point, she brought out the dessert. For the first time, a smile crossed her face as she placed it in front of him. It was her chocolate cake that was beyond the word delicious. It had always added a touch of comfort to him and she knew it. Besides, his father also loved it.

"Well, I guess you knew that would do it for me, didn't you?"

"Of course. No clichés here but a mother knows." Just knows."

After they were finished, Clay sat back and knew he had to seize th4 moment.

"I have some news you need to know."

Both of them looked at him with a mixture of puzzlement and apprehension

"Yes, what is it?" his father implored.

"The police matched some of the DNA they had."

"And?"

"It was Michael. Michael killed them."

Their reaction was a mixture of horror and disbelief and it took what seem like endless time for the room to quite enough for them to absorb what they had just heard. But after a rather disconnected conversation it was decided not to tell anyone slews at this time. But his mother would never be the same and Clay knew that.

CHAPTER TWENTY

Bitter. Utterly bitter and unbearable. Gloria and Linda's funeral were almost too much for him. Moderate sized the chapel that was used could hardly accommodate the attendees. More came from Minnesota than Clay ever thought would but the shock of the tragedy drew them here. The meeting with Bobbie and George was, as expected, very difficult, very emotional and heartbreaking.

Bobbie, immediately noting the absence of her grandson asked "where is Michael?"

Should he reveal all of this to them now, at this time, or wait until this most painful ordeal was over? As far as he knew, Gloria had not revealed to them that Michael was conceived in-utero with another man's sperm.

"You know, "stuttering to answer her," he had a meeting that night and for some reason got hung up and I have not been able to find him. Maybe he went off on a fling with his buddies."

This was as lame an answer as he could imagine but he just did not want to reveal all of this to them now. He wanted to get this over and plot out his next moves.

Later, he would ruminate on how he persevered through that double funeral. Two coffins, side by side, closed, at his request. The priest with all the accoutrements of religion and death and the insanity of it all. How we could not always understand God's plan. Clay never could, either, and now he didn't see where that made any sense at all. When it was finally over, his parents stood by his side as the coffins were carried to two waiting hearses. Two!

"Clay, honey," Carole intoned, "I cannot even begin to imagine how awful this is for you." She stopped and the emotional burden overcame her as she began to sob. Putting his arm around her, trying to maintain his equilibrium, he too, began to cry quietly with her.

"But where is Michael?" she persisted asking, confused and concerned.

"I don't know" was his repetitious answer. God, he wanted to tell her and the world that Michael had murdered his mother and half-sister. Murdered them! Raped and murdered them!

Riding in the lead hearse, with Gloria's body, Clay's mind rippled with waves of anger, grief, and planning on how he would pursue this. He was having difficulty accepting the fact that in the casket was his wife and behind them, in the other black carrier, his beautiful daughter. Carole and Ralph sat next to him, in utter and total silence, with the occasional sobs from his mother Arriving at the cemetery adorned with hundreds of crosses, and intertwined with massive mausoleums that were apparently designed to carry their occupants glory to the end of time and which Clay thought was a bit pretentious as he would have settled for cremations, they exited the hearses. A number of men and a few women had been picked by the families and a few by him to be the pall bearers. Handling the coffins carefully, they walked to a bare spot where two holes had been dug.

Clay was surprised at the large number of people who had followed them to this cemetery. From her office, from his, from Linda and Michela's school, friends of his parents, some of his childhood friends he still recognized. They were all there, forming a dolorous semicircle around those two holes and the priest who was at its apex.

It was agony waiting for this part of the ordeal to be finished. Finally, when the coffins were lowered, Clay felt as miserable as he had ever felt in his life. While he actually was uncertain if he could go on without them but the vison of that monster, that bastard Michael, burned in his brain and gave him that sense of purpose that he may not otherwise have had.

He moved quickly to Bobbie and George, standing just a few yards away, by the burial site. Their eyes reddened and the facial paleness projecting the unimaginable grief that a parent feels when they lose a child, regardless of the age.

"I am so sorry. God, I am so sorry for both of you. I know how you feel. I loved your daughter so much. And I loved my daughter as you loved yours." It was so damn difficult to say just what he had said but he felt it was said we'll under the circumstances. Bobbie nestled her head into his shoulder and George nodded his head in what must surely have been agreement although Clay was uncertain if he was cognitive of all that was going on. He seemed so distraught.

"I know, Clay" Bobbie sobbed "somehow we'll get through this. I just want them to get the bastard who did this"

And so it went that day. Dozens of family and friends saying this and that, some inane, most Clay knew was sincere but he just did not give a damn what they were saying. His mind was focused on one thing: Where is that goddamn Michael?

But he could not but notice the landscape into which his wife and daughter were eternally bound. As with many cemeteries, the lawn was manicured to a slick green carpet that seemed to reflect the sun's rays. Magnificent oak tress stood guard everywhere and the flowers had been chosen with craft and artisanship. It was simply beautiful. Too bad that everyone who was a resident here was dead. He chided himself for such a macabre thought but, actually, it was sadly true.

The four of them walked slowly away from the graves, Carole and Ralph, Billy, and George. It was as sad a moment as Clay had ever experienced. Silently they went together, the lack of words forming an invisible bond that tied them together. The implausibility of this was just too overwhelming. Carole and Ralph, of course, knew of the sperm donor bit but not Gloria's parents. Reluctant to say anything now, his mind drifted to that moment when they perused the 'catalog' and she had felt she had found the 'Superman' of sexless lovers. And then, the idea of tracking that 'superman' and what might have happened to any other artificial reproductions with other women. If any. And who was that donor? What was he really like now? Could anything about him explain what had happened to his family?

Carole and Ralph had asked Billie and George to be with them that evening. They had bonded in a fashion at the wake that was part of the Catholic rites.

As they walked, Carole brought up how she had heard from several of their Jewish friends how they would actually eat a rather large meal after a funeral, provided by friends, and forming part of the ritual called the 'shiva' which was a tribute to the departed and a time of mourning for family and friends. She suggested they might do their own abbreviated form since 'they had to eat something'. But, of course, they would simply go to a restaurant. That made sense to Clay but George was so morose that it was doubtful he cared. That would also be a good time to tell them of the epic of the artificial insemination. It needed to be out in the open as he was going to pursue this and wanted both sets of parents to be aware. He would not bring up his initial objections to her decision, however, wishing not to prejudice this whole sordid matter anymore than it seemed already to be.

They ordered food from a nearby restaurant that, while not a five star find, was adequate. Pastas and great heaping of salad seemed satisfactory and Ralph, at first reluctant but encouraged by Clay, did open two bottles of his favorite wine, cabernets from Sonoma Valley. Billie savored the food and, to Clay's surprise, consumed two full glasses of the wine. Her mood did brighten a bit, as expected. Maybe the reason she drank those two full glasses. What the hell, he thought. She deserves full four glasses. George remained sullen and distraught. His relationship with his daughter was quite profound and close, that sort of bond that is possible only between a father and daughter. He could empathize with that. Oh God, could he.

His mother served brownies stuffed with pecans, one of his favorites, along with coffee. With that and the wine, he was ready to unleash his story to her parents.

"Billie, George. There is something I need to tell you." It was how anyone would begin, he guessed. He then proceeded to weave the tale from the beginning, emphasizing Gloria's concern about having another child like Linda. He wanted to point out the major impetus for her decision. Hinting that his parents were aware of what had transpired, he hoped that there would not be any resentment and that Gloria should have included them in the loop at the get go.

Finishing, he awaited their reaction. Thee was complete silence for too long, Clay decided but he sat there, immobilized as it were, but waiting.

Billie, as he expected, was the first to respond.

"I..don't know what to say, Clay. I just don't. I do not know why she did not tell us or seek our counsel. I would have told her not to do such a thing. Period. It's been eighteen years. We did not know For God's sake." With that, her sobbing resumed, opening the dam once more.

George looked at his wife, then down at the floor, puzzlement and seething anger blending into the receptacle of his understanding. Finally, as if a statue coming to life, he gave his simple but profoundly felt agreement. "So would I have."

"She should have asked us, or told us, or both, Clay. She should have. We are totally miserable at our loss but that doesn't excuse her from what she did. We would have been unequivocally opposed, you know that?"

"Yes. I think I would have suspected as much. But she chose not to."

"Carole" Billie turned to his mother. "Did you know?"

"Yes. Clay told us. We were not pleased, either, but Gloria was determined and I did not want to interfere."

Billie, with no change in her expression, seemed to accept that.

"Who was the donor, Clay? Did you ever meet him?"

"No. Gloria did not seem inclined to do so. She was content with his pedigree. You check that out in a, well, there is no other way to out this, in a catalog, if you will. Complete with photographs. Handsome guy with a very impressive pedigree, I must admit. Gloria was instantly attracted to him or at least a facsimile of him."

"Clay, have you been able to reach Michael? I am still very confused as to where he is. How....could he miss his mother's and sister's funeral? "Billie continued to press him on that question but he was not going to reveal to them what he knew. He would take care of this himself.

"I have been trying to reach him. I don't know what has happened. I am concerned"

"Do you think...whoever did this has taken Michael? Maybe he saw it and...maybe the killer did not want to well...kill him?"

Maybe. I have thought of that. The police ae aware of his absence"

He wasn't lying to them. Stretching the truth, perhaps, but not an out and out lie. The police were aware of his absence. Were they ever!

And so it was out. The convoluted story of Gloria's great experiment....with death! But when the question of meeting the donor was raised, it started him thinking again. Were there really skeletons in his closet that should have alerted them to the hidden danger ahead?

"Clay, George and I will probably leave tomorrow. I do not want to be around in this area any longer than I need to be. I loved San Francisco but now I hate it. I will...I am. missing Gloria and Linda so much. I am very bothered by Michael's absence but I trust you to keep me posted."

"Of course. I will call or email you every day."

She smiled, perhaps, for the first time that day, and arose to come over to embrace him.

"Thank you. You were such a good husband and father. May God comfort you. I hope all of this is solved, soon."

"It will be" he assured her. And with that, good-byes were offered and he simply left. He was now determined to find put more about that donor.

CHAPTER TWENTY-ONE

But where to start? The clinic, of course. Whether they had a policy of secrecy or not seemed irrelevant to him at this time. He would force them to tell him how to contact the donor. Was he even still living or could he be reached? He had a limited time to get so much done. While his firm had offered him two weeks off and were quite compliant, he knew he could be away indefinitely. Several important items were left hanging at the time all of this happened. And would he be able to resume his previous laser-beamed concentration that had marked him as special? Hopefully, yes. But first, this.

What was that doctor's name at the Clinic where all of this had its start? Was he still practicing or, even, was he still living? Remembering that Gloria had kept records from that encounter, as well she should, he quickly drove home to start the hunt. Driving into the garage was now an ordeal. His palms moistened, his heart rate increased, sure signs, he recognized, of the anxiety associated with just the physicality of the place. If there were such things as ghosts, the forms of Gloria and Linda seemed to float throughout the house and linger, ominously, in the kitchen. The horror, the horror! It would just not go away.

Finding the cabinet where Gloria kept many of her records, he, painfully, began to thumb through them. Some, as expected, retrieved memories from years past, creating a sense of dark nostalgia while others seemed irrelevant. Finally, he found those from that clinic. Quickly turning a few pages, he did see the name he wanted: Annenberg. Yes, a Dr. Annenberg.

Reaching for the phone, he dialed the number that was on the form that Gloria kept. A pleasant female voice answered, surprisingly, as he was so habituated to the rote of a computerized greeting. After her brief introduction, thankfully, he asked if Dr. Annenberg still was practicing there

"Of course" she responded matter-of-factly. "Dr. Annenberg is our founder and still sees patients daily."

"This is very important. Is there any way I can talk to him, or better yet, can I make an appointment to see him?"

"May I ask who this concerns?"

"A very important matter. Very important, and a bit private"

"I understand. Certainly, of course. Who may I ask is calling?"

"Lawrence. Clay Lawrence."

"Yes, Dr. Annenberg can see you tomorrow afternoon at 4: 30. Would that be satisfactory, Mr. Lawrence?"

"Yes, very satisfactory."

He sat in the living room, alone, contemplative. The house still had its aura of death and loss and he was noticing his continuing discomfort of just being there. He would sell it. As soon as I take care of business, I will sell it, he told himself.

Even trying to sleep here was becoming problematic, his mind repeatedly drifting to that kitchen scene. And then the face of Michael. The bastard. He had not heard anything from the police and assumed they had not, so far, been able to locate him. Probably best not to contact them yet. Finally, reluctantly, he found some of Gloria's' sleeping meds,. took a half-dose and was able to doze off and on for a few hours jarred awake by the alarm he had set.

It was a rather typical morning for San Francisco, the fog had meandered in, it was cool, and the promise of the sun remained just a promise. Fitting, Clay thought. This day was going to be devoted to starting to clean out some of the items in the house. Removing Gloria's and Linda's clothing was much more difficult than he had anticipated. He knew that many put that task off for many weeks, if not forever. But he was determined to do it as soon as he could. Memories abounded. His mood fluctuated, first remorse, then a degree of joy when he saw the photos of Gloria and Linda when she was just a year old. It was arduous looking at them. The glossy feel resembled an imitation of life, as they certainly were at that moment. But, before he knew it, it was time to get to that clinic and his meeting with Annenberg.

Arriving at the Clinic, deja vu flooded over him. The receptionist, as he remembered, certainly was not the same. Younger and more attractive. After he reported in, she asked him to sit in the waiting room as it would be 'just a few moments' before Dr. Annenberg could see him. He fumbled with a few of the magazines, surprisingly of a recent vintage, that were neatly piled atop one of the tables. Finally, after waiting close to twenty minutes, he was ushered into his office.

Modified déjà vu here. Annenberg had aged, rather poorly at that. His previous cap of copious brown hair was not replaced by a white mat of considerably less quantity. There was a chart sitting on his desk and Annenberg was slowly browsing through its pages. Could they have retrieved Gloria's records from all of those years ago? Probably so. After shaking C lay's hand following the require introduction, he said not another word as he continued to peruse that collection of paper before him. At last, he looked up.

"Mr. Lawrence, I am aware of what has occurred in your life and I am deeply saddened. I offer my sincere sympathy."

Taken somewhat aback by this unexpected comment, Clay could only answer in the simplest of words: "thank you. I appreciate that."

"Yes. Now…why..I am not sure why you are here."

"Well, I have come to see if it's possible to meet the donor. And, do you have any information or follow-up on any other of the offspring of the women that may also have chosen him for their sperm donor."

"Why?"

"I need to know more about him."

"Why?"

Clay was uncertain how to approach this. Could he, somehow construct, a case that would touch on Michael without accusing him of any wrongdoing?

"It has to do with Michael, the offspring, of, what, that 'union'.

Annenberg's face lost its friendly mien at that remark but all he said was: "We do not usually enable the woman to meet with the donor face to face"

"The woman, in this case, is dead"

"I am aware of that, Mr. Lawrence but that still does not change the policy of this Clinic."

"Would it make any difference if I told you I think her son killed her and I need to meet with the father to get some background here?"

Okay, it was out. He felt he needed to do this to break the barrier that he was facing. By Annenberg's astonished look now, he knew he had struck a chord of some sort."

"Is that a proven fact or just your suspicion?"

"Does it make a difference?"

A span of silence followed, only a minute in actuality, but an eternity it seemed to Clay.

"No, I suppose not. I see where you are coming from, Mr. Lawrence. Look, I am not certain he is still a donor. It has been, what, sixteen years?"

"Eighteen"

"Eighteen. Well, let's see what we can find. I know what you are thinking. Did he receive some 'bad seeds' if you will. Right?"

"Correct"

"We screen our donors very thoroughly. It would be quite unusual to find skeletons in the closet. In my experience, I do not believe this sort of thing has ever come up."

"I'm sure you do. But well. I need to know. Maybe the whole world needs to know."

"Understood. Let me see what I can find out for you. And while I am very hesitant and reluctant to check on any other result of his donation, if there had been any in this clinic, I am inclined to look into that also. Yes, you are correct. I am concerned about my reputation and the standing of artificial insemination generally. As I reviewed your wife's, I'm sorry, late wife's, chart, I see the reason for her decision I need not repeat that to you. But there are many other women, most I would hazard to guess, who for whatever reason cannot get pregnant and use this method as one of the several medical science has made available to them to complete the process. For many, pregnancy is their raison d'etre. And I am truly sorry for your loss. It pains me to think that your …her son could have done anything like that, if he did. But, I will find out what I can as quietly as I can. Please leave me your contact number."

With that, he scribbled his cell phone number and left it with the receptionist. Closing the door, he walked out into the fading sunshine of a cool San Francisco afternoon, his mind churning as to what he would do when he found out anything more.

By the next afternoon, the call from Annenberg came.

"Mr. Lawrence?"

"Yes, yes. "Clay eagerly responded, very anxious indeed to hear what was next.

"I have some interesting but rather strange, even shocking, information about the donor."

"For Christ's sake, Doc, what the hell is it?" Clay's hands moistening and, again, the pounding of the heart. What did Annenberg discover and how did he do it so quickly?"

"It seems" he began slowly, too slowly for Clay, "the donor has been diagnosed as a paranoid schizophrenic. He attempted to strangle his wife and is now in the prison for the criminally insane. Whatever they call those types of prions.

Silence. Clay was both stunned and mystified, catapulted into that dark sphere of swirling emotions that characterized his last few days.

"Mr. Lawrence? Are you still on the line? I know this comes as a, well, stunner, if you will. I do not know what to say. We have no way, of course, without a previous history, to predict the ultimate health status of any of our donors"

"Of course, of course" Clay replied still stunned and a bit mystified. "I understand. I assume that the institution is in the state of California?"

"Yes. It is."

"Were you able to determine if other women used him as a donor?"

"Yes. Ordinarily, I would not give out this information. I, however, will take a chance here. There were two other women. I have no idea if they had a successful pregnancy and what happened to their offspring, if any, or what sex it was."

"Can you give me the women's names? That's all I ask. I will do the detective work myself"

"As I said, I am taking a chance here. If you will stop by the clinic again and ask my receptionist she will give you a sealed envelope with their names and the addresses we have on file. Nothing more. And, I pray justice will be done."

"Doctor, I want to thank you so much. And yes, justice will be done. I guarantee you that. This is very important to me as I've told you. I will drop by the clinic tomorrow."

Clay hung up on the call. Wonder if he feels somewhat guilty in all of this and that is the reason he is doing this. And, looks like he has his first 'bad seed'.

Clay tried to digest what he had just heard. Paranoid schizophrenia. Damn. Is Michael a schizophrenic? It never seemed that this was the problem or at least what he identified as a problem. But possible? How else to explain the unbelievable acts he had committed. But while he would leave the search for Michael up to the police, for now, he wanted to look into the other offspring of this man's sperm donation and, if at all, possible, talk to him at that institute.

Now, how can you find a needle in haystack? Both to track down those children and, ultimately, Michael if it came to that? Well, just like in the movies: find the best private eye, as they call them, you can.

A small bar that he had frequented when he was in his early twenties came to mind. Why? Well, he had met some of the wackiest characters there but some had an intimate knowledge of that 'gray zone' known collectively s the 'underworld'. He had not been there in years but maybe, just maybe, someone like that still rolled in, if the bar was still inexistence. Perhaps they would know if the best private detective might be.

The wharf. It was down by the famous Frisco wharf. Small, compact but with enough tobacco smoke to overcome the pervasive odor of beer. But the comradery he found there was unexpectedly delightful and he and his friends savored the sounds and the sights. It was a testosterone-laced bar, rarely graced by any woman except for the occasional whore looking for business. Driving down to the wharf brought back memories of his youth and for the briefest of moments eased the sight of his dead wife and daughter from his mind. But only for the briefest of moments.

And there it was! Almost as he remembered it. Amazing, he thought after all of these years. But, with the new environmental laws, only the pungent odor of beer, not of it being admixed with smoke. The clientele, however, appeared to be about what he remembered from his youth, but now there were women who did not appear to be prostitutes and some of the men enjoying a glass of wine that he never saw in here before. The modernization of George's Bar! Behind the familiar bar, silhouetted against an oversized mirror stood a tall, lean man with pure whit hair and a stubble of a beard, also pure white. He certainly looked as if he could be ol' George, now obviously showing his age. Clay walked up and fearlessly asked:

"George?"

"Yea. How can I help you? "He answered in his nostalgically gravelly deep voice.

"I don't know if you remember me or not. My name is Lawrence. Clay Lawrence."

Studying the face for a few moments, George nodded ever so faintly.

"Yea, I think so. Didn't you come in here with a bunch of guys, twenty-somethings I guess?"

"Yes. Great memory"

"It's my job to remember faces, pal. How you been?"

"Well, I need to ask a favor."

"Of me?"

"Yes. I don't know if you read about the two women who were strangled to.....strangled to death."

George now seemed in deeper concentration, trying to recall the event Clay described. His eyes narrowed as he answered.

"Yea.I think so. Why?"

"They were my wife and daughter."

"Shit. You're kidding me."

"No"

"Have they caught the son-of –a bitch that did it yet?"

"No. That's why I'm here."

"Here? What in the hell does that mean?"

For the first time in what seemed like eternity, Clay was able to project at least the semblance of a smile.

"No, it's not what you think George. I'm betting you can tell me who the best private eye around Frisco is"

George nodded.

"I see. You had me crapping in my pants for a while young man. The best in Frisco? No contest. Sam Clark."

"I knew you'd know. Does he, you know, have an office and all that or do I have to reach him in a more serpentine manner?"

"Serpentine? What's that?"

"Sorry, George. Nutty word to use. Can I reach him at his office?"

"Yes, he has an office. Nice one, too. Been there a few times. I have his card. Want it?"

"Yes, of course. I should have asked that in the first place."

He disappeared into the back room for a moment and came out with the card which he handed to Clay.

"Thanks George. By the way, do you still serve that terrific beer?"

"A Taste of the Wharf I call it. Yea. Want a glass?"

"Of course."

So Clay stood at that bar, actually enjoying the experience again, the nostalgia easing his pain.

"God, this stuff is good. I forgot how good. Look, thanks so much for your help as he laid down a twenty dollar bill."

"No problem. Hang on, I'll get your change."

"Forget that. Thanks again, I'll try to get back here a little sooner next time."

"Anytime, pal. Look, I really am sorry about your wife and daughter. What a bummer. I hope that Sam helps in whatever you're trying to do."

CHAPTER TWENTY-TWO

Sam Clark's office was a surprise. Not sure actually what to expect at the set-up of a private detective, disregarding all of those characterized on TV and in the cinema, this one was almost lavish. Amazingly, it overlooked the Bay with a view even of the Golden Gate Bridge and obviously was not a 'cheap-o'. The waiting room was paneled in a deep mahogany wood, sparkling clean with magazines of the latest vintage. Shit, Clay, thought, this has got to be expensive. Why didn't George warn me? But I did ask for the 'best'.

But Sam Clark, ah Sam Clark. He epitomized the picture of a private detective in the mind's eye. Medium height, slightly stocky, stubble of a beard, rather messy looking slacks and an opened neck shirt which definitely needed pressing. Dark brown eyes set back in a face that seemed to cover his whole head. Slightly graying, he still had an ample crop of wild hair atop that head.

"Clay Lawrence, I believe" Sam grandly greeted him with a handshake that was as firm as Clay had ever experienced. For whatever that meant.

"Listen, I know who you are That is, I am aware of the nasty, nasty crap that happened to your family. Is that why you are here?"

"Yes"

"Well, first of all, my sincere condolences"

"Thank you" Clay rather meekly responded which surprised him. Was that because of the persona of Sam Clark standing before him?

"Please sit down"

Clay sat in a large, cushioned chair directly across from a desk that was so cluttered he had no idea how anyone could find anything. What a contrast to that waiting room, he thought.

"Please fill me in"

So Clay described the events from the beginning, tracing his relationship and the seeming haughty demeanor of Michael wan what he now knew, including the story of the sperm donor.

"And the police are looking for him, correct?"

"Correct"

"So why are you here?"

"I want to find him before the police do."

"Really? Why?"

"I need to talk to him before he ends up in custody and won't talk"

"Anything else?"

"Yes. I know the names of two other women who used the donor's sperm. I want to find them and see what became of any offspring"

"All interesting and reasonable. And a bit time consuming. All right, I'm, steep, OK? Cost you a minimum of three grand. Up front.

"And if the police find him before I do?'

"No refunds. I do not operate like that.'

Clay thought for a moment. George was certain that this guy was the best. I do trust George. And, I want to find him before the police."

"All right. You're on. What do you need to know?"

"Write the check first and then we'll get started"

Wow, Clay thought. This guy would be a terrific addition to our office. But, alas, wouldn't fit in, really. Up front, he says. Well, let's take the plunge"

Extracting a blank check from his wallet, Clay calmly wrote out the check for three thousand dollars. Up front. Handing it to him, he waited.

"I'm sure you ae good for this. Did you say George recommended me?"

"Did I? Don't remember, but yes he did"

"Anyone that George sends me is good as far as I am concerned. Now, Mr. Lawrence, let's"…

"Call me Clay" he interrupted.

"OK, Clay it is. Tell me, first, about Michael and any clues I can use to find him"

Clay ran through as much as he thought he would need. He described his rapid rise through high school and his projected image as truly the "All American Boy". His relationship with Linda, or lack of one, and Gloria's utter obsession with him. And, finally, his discovery of the fate of his biological father.

Sam Clark sat impassively when Clay was through with his litany. His eyes narrowed, brow lifted in neat ripples.

"Hell of a story, Clay, hell of a story. And you think Michael got a bad gene from his father, don't you?"

"Yes, I do."

"So, this the risk of picking out a glamour boy with all the apparently right credentials. Is that the moral of this?"

"Partly."

"What will you do when I find him? I didn't say if, I said when."

"All right. You've given me some clues. And, if you will give me he names and addresses you have on those two women I'll see if I can locate them and any info about kids. Anything more?"

"Not yet. If I think of something, I'll call"

"Fair enough."

He stood, shook Clay's hand with that powerful grip.

"I will contact you everyday"

"Yes, I'd appreciate that. You have my cell number?"

"Yes, we do."

Escorting him to the door, Sam Clark seemed the epitome of the uber-confident man. Clay was impressed.

"Hope you find him soon, Sam"

Smiling broadly, Sam answered quickly: "Rest assured. Soon is the watch word here. Talk to you

For San Francisco, the weather was delightful as he left the office of Sam Clark. Bright sunshine and a very pleasant temperature. A day Gloria would delight in. The thought both saddened and angered him. Find him, Mr. Sam Clark. Find the son-of –bitch with that miserable gene. Poor Gloria. Her fantasy of engineering her next child had come to such a horrible finish. What was the lesson here? He tried not to pit this in any theological frame. But in a way, having a child for any women is a roll of the dice. Trying to hedge that roll may be more problematic than letting the chips fall where they might. But too late, too late for that philosophy now. One of these days, Clay might write a book about all of this. Something instructive, he suspected, but that was not his main goal now. Finding Michael was. And, maybe, he would see if he could meet and talk with the donor. Maybe

To his surprise, when he contacted the Correctional Bureau the next day, he found that it was possible to set up a short visit to that institute where he was incarcerated. That after the officer taking his call recognized the name and was aware of the circumstances. Clay thought that a bit strange. No further questions? But he had explained that this was part of his mission to understand the whole process of sperm banks. A two hour trip. Doable in one say he figured. Sam Clark had his cell number but it was too early for anything yet he was sure and nothing from the police. So, gulping down a second cup of coffee, he quickly went to his car and started the voyage.

Arriving at the visitor's parking area, he followed the signs to the office. Inside, he found a bare undecorated room with a large officer seated behind a half-door. No one else was in that room

As he walked up to the door, the officer continued working on something, seemingly not even noticing Clay. Then, a sudden "Yes, what can I do for you?"

"I had called about seeing a Mr. Gerald Carpenter. My name is Clay Lawrence."

"One moment, Mr. Lawrence. Take a seat while I check this out."

Clay turned, found a very uncomfortable wooden chair and simply did just that. Waited. No magazines, papers nothing. He felt it would be inappropriate to use his cell but kept it on just in case.

Finally, the seemingly weary officer asked him to come to the window.

"Mr. Lawrence. We have arranged for you to meet Mr. Carpenter in a section reserved for this sort of thing. He will be across from you with a glass window between. A button is available if any assistance is needed. If you will enter hat door to the left of you, I will take you to the room."

"Thank you, officer" Clay obediently responded.

As he opened the door, he was surprised with the size of the man. At least six feet three he estimated and a bunch of pounds to go with it. No messing with this guy.

He followed him down a corridor, took a turn to the right and was ushered into a brightly lit room with a single chair across from a windowed panel. Already seated was the man he wanted to meet.

A familiar face, although it had been over sixteen years since he and Gloria had viewed his snapshot in that 'catalog'. Now, thinning hair, sprinkled with streams of gray, thinner, eyes more set back it seemed. A face of what, depression? Schizophrenia? Whatever that was supposed to show as.

Taking a chair across from Gerald Carpenter, he looked at him with a wary eye.

"Hello, Mr. Carpenter?"

A hiatus of silenced followed by a curt "Yes"

"Mr. Carpenter, my name is Clay Lawrence."

"So?"

"My wife chose you as the sperm donor sixteen years ago."

A strange visage confronted Clay. Different. Eerie. A bit frightening.

"She did? You will have to excuse me, Mr…Mr.."

"Lawrence"

"Lawrence. Yes, Lawrence. Memory a bit shot these days. Yes, I can remember doing that crazy thing." A faint smile now appeared. "Seems crazy now. Crazy. Not a word I am supposed to use. So, why are you here? Want me to do it again? "With that a bizarre cackle. This was not going to be easy, Clay assumed.

"She conceived a son. Turned out to be a handsome kid. Smart as hell Great athlete."

"Well, isn't that something? So, you here just to tell me that?"

"He raped and killed her and my daughter, his half-sister"

Gerald Carpenter just looked at him with a very blank state. Very inappropriate response.

"Well, isn't that a son-of-a bitch. I am sorry, Mr. Lawrence. But what has that got to do with me. I have My own problems"

"Well, I think you gave him a bad gene. A killer gene, if you will."

Suddenly, unexpectedly, there was a complete reversal. Gerald Carpenter started to actually weep.

"I am sorry, really. So sorry. You know, Mr. Lawrence, I graduated from Harvard with honors. Went on to a successful career in finance San Francisco. Married a wonderful woman, smart as hell, beautiful. Then, then, these weird thoughts and sights started to cram into my brain. I had some of that when I was younger but …this was more. I tried to kill my wife, Mr. Lawrence. My beautiful, smart wife. She barely survived. Now, I am charged with attempted murder and they tell me I am a schizophrenic. On a bunch of meds. My head gets real cloudy sometimes."

"Did you tell any of this to the Sperm Bank?'

"Tell them what?"

"Your thoughts, you know what you just told me"

"I didn't have much of that then. I hadn't seen anyone and I thought I was in good health. No, I did not tell them anything like that."

Clay tried to digest that answer.

"Did you and your wife any children?"

"No. She didn't want any kids. I don't know why"

Clay wondered if his smart wife had begun to notice certain traits in him that made that decision for her.

"Is your wife all right"

"She…suffered neurological damage. I…"

Clay decided that it was time to end this meeting. He had met the man. What did he learn? Probably was a very brilliant guy whose wiring went haywire. No kids thought. He needed to see if those women bore any of his offspring and what happened to them. Hopefully, Sam Clark can track them.

"Thank you, Mr. Carpenter. I appreciate you meeting with me. I hope you get well soon. Also, hope your wife gets better."

Gerald Carpenter looked down. Nothing. Then a single "Thanks"

It was over. Was this really a case of a killer gene? He still was convinced it was.

CHAPTER TWENTY-THREE

He had sent Sam a number of items and answers that he had requested. Some of it made no sense to Clay but, what the hell, he was the big private eye, not him. He had spent the next few days after visiting Gerald Carpenter sorting things around the house. He knew he would sell it. Too many horrible memories, just too many. Part of the time, he had snuck into the office to catch up on a few items. The waves of sympathy inside that office were a bit overwhelming but he knew he had to deal with them sooner or later. Again, he was told he did not feel he had to return any sooner than when he was ready.

When that phone rang that Thursday afternoon, he had just left the office after a brief stopover and decided to simply stroll around the block before driving to a small sea food restaurant he and Gloria frequented at Fisherman's Wharf. He had not been there since her death but wanted to experience the feel and smell of it again, hoping to meet her ghost there perhaps. The Wharf was clearly the spot he cherished most in this city, cherished it since he first went as a teenager all those years ago.

Recognizing Sam's voice immediately, he felt that sense of expectation and the unknown.

"Mr. Lawrence?"

"Yes, Sam. I recognize your voice. Ys, its Clay Lawrence. What's up?"

"Several things to report. As you can imagine, we have been very busy these past few days with your requests. But I have an excellent team. First, we were able to trace both of those women's whereabouts. Much to discuss. So, why don't you drop in here. And, I think we are close to pinpointing where Michael may be."

Clay was actually stunned and surprised by all of that. It's as if the impossible was conquered in just a few days! Incredible!

"Wow" was his immediate response, more disbelieving than anything.

"Yes, I thought you would be pleased with our progress. Again, when would it be convenient for you to come back to see me?"

"I am free this afternoon and, well, anytime tomorrow"

"How does four this afternoon sound?"

"Great. I'll be there"

"Good, see you then. I think you will be intrigued with what we discovered"

"I already am"

It was two already. Clay decided to simply stay put at the restaurant since his table was on the water and he was in a very contemplative mood. What would Sam Clark reveal to him? Would it be a shock? There was a moral in all of this but he was still constructing it. One part was certain: gambling with Nature meant more than just the roll of the dice. Particularly if you stepped out of the perennial boundaries which Gloria had done? But how would you have predicted all of this?

No way. Or was there? The water brought its usual tranquility to him for which Clay was always grateful and the contemplation ended there. Glancing at his watch, he decided it was to time to head over to Sam Clark's and discover the discovery.

It was just before four when he walked into that office. God, that waiting room was so damn magnificent! Too bad Sam's office didn't duplicate its orderliness and splendor.

"Mr. Lawrence" came the voice from the front desk.

"Yes" boy, I guess they were expecting me all right.

"Mr. Clark is free. Please follow me and I'll take you to his office."

"Great"

Clay once again followed the path to Sam's office. As the door opened, the familiar figure at behind that cluttered desk. Looking up, he greeted him and bade him sit in the chair across from him.

"Well, Mr. Lawrence."

Clay interrupted "please call me Clay"

"Certainly. Clay it is. To begin, we did trace the two women who also received sperm from your man. One is from San Bernardino, the other from Mountain View. Let's start with the one from San Bernardino. She bore a son approximately nine months after her visit to the Bank. One would assume that was the result of the donation. Now, this kid, this kid is a little like you described Michael. Very smart. Top athlete. President of his senior class. And, the kicker. He is in the penitentiary for rape."

"You are kidding me?" Clay responded in astonishment.

"No. That gene again"

"Did he…kill anyone or was it just, just is a funny word here, but was it just rape?'

"Just rape. But this was the second time. He may have attempted to do more but the woman fought him off."

"And the second woman?"

"Yes. The one from Mountain view. She delivered a daughter. A little tougher to get the data here but my guy says she is in no legal trouble but has been disciplined several times at her high school and has been a problem with control. She is under mental health care but I cannot get any more than that. Still in school and is a very high achiever but has that character defect. Goes along with your theory, Clay, but not a killer. Yet."

Clay sat immobilized. Absolutely mind-boggling. Astonishing. Who would have guessed something like this? You couldn't write a more bizarre script if you tried.

"Clay? Are you all right?"

"Yes, I'm sorry, Sam. This is all so unbelievable. Just unbelievable. Don't you think?"

Clay wasn't certain one should ask a private detective, particularly one of Sam Clark's stature, such a question. He watched as Sam seemed to be forming an answer.

"Yes, Clay. I agree. I am not sure I ever investigated a case quite like this. I mean the interesting implications you have constructed and we have found. But I also want to tell you that I think we have a bead on where your son, I guess we can say that, might be.

"Really?"

"Yes.'

"Where is he?"

"We think he's holed up in a motel in Flagstaff, Arizona"

"Flagstaff?"

"Yes, Flagstaff"

"Can you tell me which one?"

"We think he is in a Motel 6. One at West Woodlands Village. Location is by I-40 and US 180"

Clay quickly wrote that down.

"Thank you, Sam. You were swift and thorough. I appreciate it.'

"That's my job, Clay. Look, I can only imagine how you feel. I don't know what you are up to here but take my advice. Don't do anything stupid. You will regret it."

"I appreciate that, Sam. I really do. Again, thank you for the competence you've showed me. Money well spent."

Clay walked out of the office, nodded to the receptionist and got into his car. He had worked out his next move. He still had not heard from the police. Good. I want him first. He turned on the engine, confident in his mission, and headed downtown. His next stop was at a gun store he had often noticed but had quickly ignored. Not this time. It felt odd walking into that store. Glistening handguns showcased behind glass enclosures, rifles mounted on the wall, a whole selection of ammunition. Here in San Francisco. Amazing!

A giant of a man was behind the counter. No one else was in the store.

"Yes, Sir. Can I help you?"

On his way here, Clay had rehearsed what he would say. "Yes, I need something for the house. We've been hit with a few robberies in our neighborhood lately and I want protection. I don't want to rely on waiting for the police to respond if something happens."

"As you shouldn't. Yes, we have a nice line of revolvers for home protection."

The giant, or Henry as he had introduced himself, ran through a litany of the features of a revolver.

None of this made much sense with Clay but he finally picked one that was small but carried six bullets.

"Now, if you will give me a few moments I need to run a background check before I can sell you any gun. May I see your driver's license, please?"

"Certainly" Clay responded as he pulled out his wallet and took out his license. Hopefully, he wouldn't associate his name with the recent events nor anything come up on his background check about this. He doubted that but you never know.

"Thank you."

Henry sat down at a computer behind him. In what seemed an interminable amount of time but actually was not, he arose and returned to Clay.

"Nothing here, Buddy. Clean as a whistle. So, it's your gun if you want it."

Using cash, he thanked Henry listening as he was instructed in the fundamentals of the revolver and received a suggestion to take practice at a shooting range he would recommend. He decided not to go to that range as he might not rally use the gun and Henry had showed him the workings of it. But he wanted it, just in case. This, this Michael this aberration was more than he had ever imagined.

Getting back into his car, with the revolver on safety he opened the glove compartment and placed it there. He set his GPS for Motel 6t in Flagstaff and headed east, the sun setting on his back, the cool evening air blowing in the window, a future that was uncertain but one he determined to map out on his terms.

CHAPTER TWENTY-FOUR

Heading towards Interstate 40 which would ultimately take him into Flagstaff, Clay reviewed all that had gone on in the past eighteen years since Michael was born. Regret, utter regret. Why had he not resisted her insistence that she wanted an anonymous donor to bypass the possibility that it was his genes that had created Linda? Tricking Nature was what it was. Her audacity, her, well, conceit, now came into a burning focus but was instantly tempered by the vison of her lying nude on the kitchen floor, strangled. But he knew, everyone knows, that you cannot go back, you cannot live a life of regret. It just doesn't work that way. As he drove out from vista of San Francisco and entered the more supine greenery of Central California, he found it to be an emollient covering his horrible wounds. Traffic was sparse, of course, away from the peninsula which gave him a wondrous feeling of freedom, if you could call it that. What would he do when he confronted that monster? Was he now also schizophrenic like his father? Should that emit sympathy from him? Would it contain his profound anger? But now, the scenery was morphing into the tan patina of dessert. Spread wide apart, with nothing but highway between them he found these small towns quaint and inviting, so different from the gyrating pace of Frisco.

It was well into the evening hours when he decided to stop at a pleasant looking diner on the western outskirts of Barstow. Now, just a few hour from Flagstaff, he did not want to be hungry when he arrived at the motel. The diner was brightly lit with murals depicting what he thought was Navajo life. But very clean looking. Taking a small booth, he was given the menu which had an interesting variety of western style fare as well as others. A middle-aged waitress, attractive but wearing a wedding band, came out to take his order.

Looking up, he was quick to ask if they served liquor, not taking the time to glance behind him which revealed a fairly well- stocked bar with an array of bottles.

"Yes, sir. A good one, too"

"Well, how about some Crown Royal on the rocks""

"Double?"

"No, need to keep my head together."

Laughing, she told him she understood.

Why he felt serene here, he did not know. But he did. Maybe the solitude, the freshness of this place, the remoteness. He was hungry and that played a role. Returning with his drink, she placed it in front of him and ran through some of the specials. He settled on an eight ounce filet fixed in the 'western style' as she put it. Cottage fried potatoes accompanied that selection, which being one of his favorites, he pounced on. She fairly frothed over their Caesar salad to which he also instantly acceded. Sipping on the whiskey, in the face of his relative food abstinence for a number of hours, a feeling of calm and a slightly floating feeling arrived much earlier than he would have expected.

Amazingly, his anger seemed to fade a b it and more pleasant memories of their family in better times settled in. At one time, he had actually been proud of Michael but as he grew older, his personality became more stringent and condescending. But always, always, he fantasized what would have been

If Gloria had never considered a surrogate donor and they had another child the 'natural way'. The lesson kept repeating itself like a never ending echo throbbing through his brain. This kind of thing would go on, he knew, but to avoid the risk of producing a child a bit less than one of his parents would have wished seemed, well, unnatural. Not immoral. Unnatural. And in this case, catastrophic. Maybe the risk of choosing a complete stranger based only on a résumé was the bigger danger.

The arrival of his salad, a bit mammoth as she had predicted, interrupted his reverie.

"Now that is what I would call a salad "he jokingly remarked

"Yep. As I said. Your meal will be out shortly."

He enjoyed that salad more than he thought he would. Maybe it was his hunger, maybe the effect of the drink which he had now finished. But it did taste good, probably with the dressing which was quite unique in his experience. Most of it was gone when his dinner arrived. 'Western style' amounted to a very tender steak that had been flavored with rather tangy coating and in turn was covered with a pile of mushrooms in its own sauce. The potatoes were crisp and plentiful. All in all, it turned out to be more of a dining experience than he had anticipated. When he had finished he found himself able to inquire as to the dessert menu, which he often skipped when dinging out. But tonight, he chose a piece of apple pie topped off with ice cream, the whole works! The thought of this being his 'last meal' suddenly crossed his mind, bring an unwelcomed sense of despair and fear, and while only momentary, was all too real.

"More coffee, sir?" prodded the waitress in her gentle voice which broke that train of thought.

"Yes, I think so.' He answered, calculating he would need the extra caffeine if he was to complete the drive tonight which he fully intended to do.

Finished, he asked for his bill and graciously added a 25% gratuity for that waitress who seemed so interested that things went well for him.

So now, on to Flagstaff, listening to the soothing computerized female voce that was guiding him there. It was almost 8:00 and the last remnants of sunshine cast its glorious shadow onto the surrounding desert and hills. The magnificence of Nature never failed to amaze him and he was fascinated by all of this. He had not been in this area for years, so different than the fly-overs that were so common to him

Finally reaching Flagstaff, he turned onto the South Beulah Blvd ramp, proceeding to South Woodland Village and the pounding light of Motel 6. As he drove into the parking lot, he instantly recognized Michael's car. Why hadn't the police sniffed this out before Sam? Mystery to me, he thought. So he was still here. What had happened in the interval? Had he caused more mischief? Was he registered as Michael Lawrence? He almost had to be if they asked for some form of identification. He parked away from that car, turned off the motor and walked towards the office to somehow get his room number.

An Older man was sitting quietly behind a reception desk that seemed a bit worn. Looking up, he quickly rose to his feet.

"Yes sir, may I help you?"

"Hope so. My name is Clay Lawrence and my son forgot to give me his room number. I cannot get his cell for some reason and I was supposed to meet him here. Michael Lawrence. His name is Michael."

The older man squinted, asked for his driver's license, still hesitated but finally seemed convinced. Looking over a list of rooms, he answered him.

"235.Upstairs, near the elevator."

Thanks so much."

"Will you be needing a room?" the old man asked.

"Maybe. Let me talk to Michael first"

Walking just a few steps, he pushed the up button and slipped into the elevator as the door opened. Pressing floor two, feeling the revolver in his coat pocket, he pressed floor two, and went to meet his destiny.

CHAPTER TWENTY-FIVE

As the door opened, he looked at the room numbers listed in front of him. Evens to the right, odds to the left. Turning to the right, and construing that he probably was in his room, considering the car was parked outside, Clay had to decide on that spot how he would approach this. If he just announced himself, would Michael attempt to flee? If he knocked on the door without giving away who he it was and then tried to force his way in, would Michael attack him? He was, of course, a young, muscled athlete and could he hold his own. Only one way. Pull out the revolver. That should be an entry ticket.

Nobody was in view, he carefully noted, as he approached the room and knocked.

Nothing. Then: "Yes? Who is it?"

Trying to disguise his voice, Clay answered that it was the manager and he had a package that was addressed to this room but with no name and he was confused and thought he needed to look at it. That id it. As the door opened, Clay held the revolver in his hand and pointed it straight ahead.

"Don't close that door, Michael, or I swear I'll shoot your fucking ass right now."

Stunned, Michael stood still for what seemed like an eternity but did not try to force the door closed. Clay pushed his way in.'

"How. did you find me?" Michael meekly asked.

"That's irrelevant. I did find you, you bastard. Now, sit down. I've got some things to tell you."

With the sight of that gun in front of him, Michael did as Clay asked. Did he really believe Clay would shoot if he tried to wrestle it from him? He was uncertain at that point how to handle this but he, of course, would have it figured out in a short period of time.

"Al right. Now that you are seated, and, don't try anything funny, really,. Don't. I am going to tell you that I am not your biological father." There was no hesitation in that approach. He watched as Michael's face gelled into one of surprise and maybe hate.

"What the hell does that mean?" he asked.

"Just what I said, your mother, the one you assaulted and strangled, was concerned we might have another child like

Linda. She wanted some brilliant kid who would save the world. Somehow, I let her go ahead worth that ridiculous fantasy. It works by going through a stupid catalogue of heroes and trying to pick a winner. They use donated sperm and presto! Superman arrives. Instead, we got you."

Clay thought Michael was going to bolt at him and with as steady a hand as he could muster, held the gun pointed in his direction.

"Stay seated young man. I am not finished. All right, that is the basics. So, after your little escapade in the kitchen, I found your biological father. And guess what? I found him in prison. He is a paranoid schizophrenic. And guess what, you son-of a-bitch, he tried to strangle his wife."

Michael sat immobile Clay suspected he was absorbing all of this. Did the revelation of his father being a schizophrenic register and if so, what would it do to him, if anything?

"Why in the hell did you do what you did? Your mother adored you and was so proud"

Clay watched as Michael's expression changed from one of frozen immobility to one where he thought he detected a wry smile.

"You are one of the bastards who ae part of the wall sanding on my way. My mother, not a bad soul I guess but she too was in my way. She was trying to make me in her image. And that fucking sister of mine or whatever she was, the stupid bitch reflected her stupidity onto me, me, who can run races around just about everyone. And now…

you..you, not even my father. I should have suspected as much. Never liked me, did you? I was smarter and stronger than you. Wimp. Took that stupid sister's side over me. I knew, well, I think I am going to do to you what I did to that scheming wife and stupid daughter of yours. You won't shoot me. You're too much of a wimp."

And with that, he suddenly lurched. Pulling the trigger was easier than he thought it would be. And louder. Michael fell instantly, without a sound, the tickle of blood oozing from his chest. Clay was tempted to keep shooting but it seemed obvious he was dead. That loud noise had quickly summoned the man from the desk. As he opened the door, Clay dropped the revolver.

"He's dead. You can call the police"